INFINITE OPPORTUNITIES

By

CECELIA FRANCES PAGE

iUniverse, Inc.
New York Bloomington

INFINITE OPPORTUNITIES

iUniverse books may be ordered through booksellers or by contacting:

iUniverse
1663 Liberty Drive
Bloomington, IN 47403
www.iuniverse.com
1-800-Authors (1-800-288-4677)

ISBN: 978-1-4401-7962-4 (pbk)
ISBN: 978-1-4401-7963-1 (ebook)

Printed in the United States of America

iUniverse rev. date: 11/3/09

Contents

Preface

INFINITE OPPORTUNITIES is a book of seventy short stories and articles about many worthwhile topics and issues. TRAVEL TOPICS are Indonesian Charms, Weekend Adventures, Learning About Scandinavia and Knowledge About the Philippine Islands. NATURE TOPICS are Gardening Techniques, Learning About Bees, Eucalyptus Trees, At the Lagoon, Life of Wild Animals, Forest Wonders and Destinations Into Outer Space.

ADVENTURE TOPICS are Mountain Climbing, Skiing Competition, Settling in Pioneer Country, Summer Delights, Unusual Experiences and Other Dimensions. HEALTH TOPICS are Breathing Incense, A Positive Outlook on Life, Reverse The Aging Process and Remedies for Diseases. PHILOSOPHICAL TOPICS are Why People Gossip, Joyous Living, Séances, Meditation, Self Responsibility, Moments of Ecstasy and Purposeful Living. SOCIAL TOPICS are Telephone Friends, Cafeteria Experience, The Assembly, Sunset Boulevard, Foster Parents, An Interesting Conversation, Acting on Impulses, Dealing With Bi-polar People and Working to Promote World Peace.

SPECIAL OCCASIONS are Outdoor Theaters, The Assembly, Special Holidays, Strawberry Bonanza, Extravaganzas, Dressing Up, The Big Celebration and Fiesta Time. CREATIVE EXPERIENCES are Creative Endeavors, Whistling, Director of Stage plays and Screenplays, Making Props and Sets, Preparing Pastries, Playing an Organ, Producing Leather Goods, Exotic Melodies, Flower Bouquets, Ways to Prepare Eggs, OTHER TOPICS are Driving a Car, The Bermuda Triangle, The Winery, The Colony, Paradise Valley, Rolling Stones and Skyscraper Majesty. All these many topics are stimulating and worth reading.

About The Author

Cecelia Frances Page began writing at age 19. Cecelia received a B.A. and M.A. in Education. She focused in Speech, English, Drama and Psychology. Cecelia has written 49 books. She published 8 books on her own. 37 books are published by iUniverse Publications. Cecelia is an author, educator, philosopher, musician, artist, photographer and voice and piano teacher. She is a vocal soloist. Cecelia Frances Page continues to write worthwhile books to inspire her readers.

Cecelia Frances Page has published five, original screenplays and three, original, poetry books. The original screenplays are entitled WALKING IN THE LIGHT, FLASHBACKS, CELESTIAL CONNECTIONS I and II and ADVENTURES IN LEMURIA I and II. The three, original, poetry books are entitled COSMIC DIMENSIONS, VIVID IMPRESSIONS and SIGNIFICANT INTROSPECTIONS. Cecelia Frances Page has written over five hundred, original poems. Several of her poems are published in THE WORLD'S BEST POEMS OF 2004 and 2005.

Cecelia Frances Page's books published by iUniverse Publishers are entitled: WESTWARD PURSUIT, OPPORTUNE TIMES, IMAGINE IF…., FORTUNATELY, MYSTICAL REALITIES, MAGNIFICENT CELESTIAL JOURNEYS, EXTRAORDINARY ENCOUNTERS, BRILLIANT CANDOR, EXPAND YOUR AWARENESS, SEEK ENLIGHTENMENT WITHIN, VIVID MEMORIES OF HALCYON, AWAKEN TO SPIRITUAL ILLUMINATION, ADVENTURES ON ANCIENT CONTINENTS, PATHWAYS TO SPIRITUAL REALIZATION, CELESTIAL CONNECTIONS, PHENOMENAL EXPERIENCES, CELESTIAL BEINGS FROM OUTER SPACE, AWESOME EPISODES, INCREDIBLE TIMES, INTERPRETATIONS OF LIFE, NEW PERSPECTIVES, TREMENDOUS MOMENTS, AMAZING STORIES AND ARTICLES, HORIZONS BEYOND, FASCINATING TOPICS, CERTAIN PEOPLE MAKE A DIFFERENCE, ADVENTUROUS EXPERIENCES, THE FUTURE AGE BEYOND THE NEW AGE MOVEMENT, POWER OF CREATIVE AND WORTHWHILE LIVING, EXTRATERRESTRIAL CIVILIZATIONS ON EARTH, RELEVANT INTERESTS, REMARKABLE WORLD TRAVELS, IMPRESSIONABLE OCCURRENCES, INFINITE OPPORTUNITIES, RANDOM SELECTIONS and more.

ONE

New Opportunities

New opportunities exist for many people. Each opportunity helps to enrich an individual's life. Social opportunities help us meet new friends and acquaintances which enhance our lives. We can have a happier life when we experience new opportunities.

Shelley Chesterfield lived in a small, quiet, conservative town. She had little opportunity to improve her life. She attended the local elementary school and high school. She wanted to go away to college. She had just graduated from high school.

There were colleges in nearby cities such as Chicago, Boston and New York City. Shelley decided to fill out applications to different universities. Shelley was a top student in elementary school and high school. She hoped to be accepted at one or more of the universities in the cities. Such an opportunity would help her receive an excellent higher education.

Within two months Shelley received responses to her applications. She was accepted at the University of New York in New York City. Shelley knew this would give her a new opportunity to improve her life. She planned to become a botanist. She would major in Botany.

Shelley wrote to the Registrar of Enrollment to let them know that she had accepted the enrollment at the University of New York for the coming Fall term of that year. Shelley was very excited about her new opportunity to attend the University of New York City.

In August of that year Shelley Chesterfield packed her clothes and other necessary belongings and items in several suitcases. She took Amtrak from her home town to New York City after saying goodbye to her parents. She had worked every summer from the age of 12 to earn money for her college education. It took her 20 hours to get to New York City. She arrived the next day by 11 a.m. at the New York City Amtrak Station.

Shelley didn't know anyone in New York City. She had called a number of rental agencies to locate a place for her to stay before she came to New York City. Once Shelley was in the New York Amtrak Station she collected her luggage. She went to a public telephone and phoned a rental agency who had arranged an apartment for her to rent.

Shelley took a public bus to the address of her new rental apartment. The rental agent was there waiting for her arrival. He handed her the apartment key after she signed a rental agreement and paid for the first month's rent plus a security deposit. Shelley was given a copy of the rental agreement. She was going to live close to the University of New York City in one of the avenues. She would ride a bicycle to the university.

Bicycle shops were listed in the telephone book. Once Shelley was settled in her furnished apartment she went to a bicycle shop to select and purchase a bicycle. She also bought a chain with a lock to protect her bicycle from robberies. She rode her new bicycle back to her apartment. She placed her bicycle in her apartment so she could keep track of it. She wasn't taking any chances.

University classes would start on the next Tuesday after registration on Monday of that week. Shelley registered for four classes on Monday. She went to the university book store to buy required text books for her college courses. She signed up for General Education courses in English, Biology, Social Sciences and Mathematics. She would take 12 units the first quarter. She had already taken the entrance exam by mail in her home town. She had passed the entrance exam. This is why she was accepted at the University of New York City.

After Shelley enrolled in four General Education courses she began attending her classes on Tuesday. She took her required textbooks to her assigned classes after she found out what textbooks to buy. She had the opportunity to take lecture notes which she recorded in notebooks. Shelley studied her lecture notes and read her textbooks to prepare for course exams. She also participated in study groups to discuss lecture notes and textbook readings to prepare for exams.

Shelley attended the University of New York City for seven years. She completed her Botany major and Masters degree in Botany. She had the opportunity to draw diagrams and illustrations of many plants. She labeled her drawings carefully.

She gathered many plant specimens and kept them in larger folders. She was able to help discover new plants.

Shelley attended Broadway Shows and went to Chinatown museums, galleries, exotic restaurants and theaters in New York City during the seven years she lived there. She also went to operas because she appreciated opera music.

Once Shelley graduated with a B.S. and M.S. in Botany she searched for a job in the field of Botany. She had received a teaching certificate in Botany. She applied for teaching positions around the U.S.A. After six months of job hunting Shelley was offered a position at a junior college in Seattle, Washington for the coming fall quarter.

With this new opportunity to teach junior college in Seattle, Washington, Shelley was able to present her plant collections and drawings. She took her college students on field trips to collect plant specimens to study. Shelley continued to teach Botany at the junior college for many years. She was a successful Botany teacher. She appreciated her opportunity to receive a B.S. and M.S. in Botany and to be able to teach Botany at a junior college.

Shelley became familiar with the cultural and social opportunities in Seattle, Washington. She went to the well known Space Needle and went to the top. The Space Needle swirled around revolving regularly. She was able to see for miles. She enjoyed the spectacular view of Seattle. Shelley enjoyed going to art exhibits and galleries, theaters and the Opera House in Seattle.

Shelley met many interesting people in Seattle over the many years she lived there. She eventually met a colleague who specialized in Micro-biotic Science. She dated this charming man, who had a Ph.D in Micro-biotics. He was a university professor at the University of Seattle. After several years of dating him they were married. Shelley and her husband Mark were happily married. In time, they raised three children. Shelley was glad that she had many new opportunities in her life.

— TWO —

Indonesian Charms

Indonesia is known as the magnificent Spice Islands in the East Indies which provided Europe with exotic spices and priceless treasures. Indonesia has a variety of landscapes and lifestyles. Indonesia has oil. As a result, Indonesia has developed into a prosperous nation.

East Timor withdrew from Indonesia in 1977 which helped cause political unrest. Today, Indonesia is in an economic crisis. Indonesia is the largest archipelago in the world. Indonesia is a nation of 13,670 islands stretching over 3,200 miles between the Indian and Pacific oceans, a distance greater than the width of the United States. Its total land area is almost three times the size of Texas or two and one-half times the size of Australia.

Indonesia is called Tanah Air Kita which means "Our Nation of Land and Water" because 80 percent of this country's territory is in fact water. Indonesia's five main

islands are Sumatra, Java, Kalimantan, Borneo, Sulawest and Irian Jaya. Only 6,670 of Indonesia's islands are inhabited. These vary in size from rocky outcrops to larger islands. However, many islands are so small they do not even have a name.

The Indonesian islands were formed during the Miocene period about 15 million years ago. Most of Indonesia's volcanoes are part of the Sunda arc, which is a 1,864 mile long line of volcanoes extending from northern Sumatra to the Banda Sea. Most of these volcanoes are the result of subduction of the Australian Plate beneath the Eurasia Plate.

Indonesia is located in one of the most volatile geological regions in the world. The mountainous spine, which runs right through the archipelago, contains hundreds of volcanoes, 220 of which are still active, with the 76 recorded eruptions. There are conical-shaped mountains, which often have smoke billowing from them. The ash and debris regularly spewed out of the volcanoes are washed down and deposited in the alluvial plains. This whitish ash deposit is so rich in chemicals that it has produced some of the most fertile soils in the world. Three rice crops can be produced in a year without the use of fertilizers, providing the staple food for one of the most populous countries in the world.

In 1850 a British naturalist named Alfred Russell explored Indonesia. He found out that there were clear boundaries within which one could find plants and animals typical of the Asian (or Oriental) mainland, those that were associated with Australia and another zone that had another category of plants and animals. One possible explanation for these boundaries is that during the last Ice Age, sea levels dropped so low that the islands on the Sunda Shelf---Borneo, Sumatra, Java, Bali and some islands on the Lesser Sundra chain---were joined to the Asian mainland. The Indonesian islands may have once formed a single land mass that was connected to the mainland. New Guinea fits neatly into northern Australia. It sits on the Sahul Shelf which is a northeastern extension of the Australian continental mass. This may be why animals from Australia such as the tree kangaroos and wallabies can be found here.

In between the Sunda Shelf and the Sahul Shelf lies the Lesser Sunda region. A unique feature of the region is that it contains animal species not found anywhere else in Indonesia. The Lesser Sunda regions are separated from the other islands by deep sea trenches which are 24,442 feet at their deepest. When sea levels fell during the last Ice Age this region remained isolated. Rhinoceroses live in Indonesia.

Since Indonesia is near the equator, it experiences hot and humid weather all year long. Indonesia has only two seasons. The dry season lasts from June to September. The wet season is from December to March. During the dry season Indonesia has winds from the southeast. The wet monsoon season brings rain from northeasterly winds, which are moisture-laden which come from the South China Sea. Tremendous walls of water explode from the sky so that it is like standing under a huge waterfall. Rainfalls can occur at any time of the year and it is even wetter in the mountainous areas, where it becomes hard to distinguish between the wet and the dry seasons. It never seems to stop raining in Sumatra and Kalimantan.

Temperatures in Indonesia average about 81 degrees F. (27 degrees C) and vary only according to altitude. Coastal plains experience temperatures of 80 degrees F (27 degrees C). As you go higher the temperature drops by 2 degrees F (l.l. degrees C) every 656 feet (200 m), resulting in a very pleasant 68 degrees to 72 degrees F in the highlands.

Many Indonesians frequently go to the mountains to spend their vacations "cooling off" from the heat of the lowlands. The famous Mandala Mountain in Irian Jaya is snowcapped even though it is on the equator.

Most of Indonesia is covered in evergreen equatorial rain forests. There are mangrove swamps with their looping aerial roots in eastern Sumatra and large tracts of arid savannah grassland in the Lesser Sunda islands. At higher altitudes there are alpine meadows with chestnut, laurel and oak trees that are commonly found in countries with temperate rather than tropical climates.

The abundant rainfall and high humidity have produced some of the densest forests in the world. These forests are also self-fertilizing because the plants decompose and form rich humus very quickly after they die. Indonesian flora is exotic and incredibly diverse with over 40,000 species recorded to date. About 6,000 species of plants are known to be used directly or indirectly. Indonesia has some of the world's richest timber resources and the largest concentration of tropical hardwood. Indonesia has more than 3,000 valuable tree species including durian, teak, ironwood, rattan, ebony, sandalwood, camphor, clove and nutmeg. Kalimantan and Java are centers for timber operations, where meranti and teak grow respectively.

Among Indonesia's flowers and plants are some 5,000 species of orchids ranging from the largest of all orchids to the tiny

Taentophyllum, which is edible and used in medical preparation and handicrafts.

One of the largest flowers in the world Rafflesia Arnoldit grows in Indonesia. Indonesia has a variety of wildlife. It is home to 12 percent of the world's mammal species, 16 percent of the world's amphibian and reptile species, 17 percent of the world's bird species and 25 percent of the world's species of fish.

Indonesia's birds and animals include the one-horned rhinoceros of Java; the brilliantly colored bird of paradise that cannot fly; the tiny Lesser mouse deer which stands one foot tall; the ancient Komodo dragon; the Bali starling with silky snow-white features, black wing and tail tips; tigers, tapirs, marsupials such as bandicoots and cuscuses, peacocks, kuau, anoa and numerous other animals.

The single-horned Sumatran rhinoceros are confined to the Kulon Peninsula National Park in Java. Another endangered species is the orangutan from Borneo and Sumatra. Orangutan rehabilitation centers have been set up at Mount Leuser National Park in northern Sumatra and in a game preserve in southern Kalimantan. Other endangered animals in Indonesia include the siamang, Javan rhinoceros, banteng, Malay tapir, tiger, Sun bear, leopard and elephant.

Indonesia's insect kingdom is just as fascinating including giant walking sticks, which can grow as long as 8 inches, walking leaves, huge atlas beetles and lovely luna moths. Indonesia's complex coral reefs and marine ecosystems have rich marine life, ranging from big game fish---such as marlins, tuna, barracuda and Wahoo to whales, hammerhead sharks and manta rays.

The Komodo dragon is the largest lizard in the world. They are relatives of the dinosaurs. Komodo dragons have lived in Indonesia for millions of years on the island of Komodo and Rinea. These huge lizards can measure up to 10 feet and weigh 300 pounds. They have long scaly bodies supported on short, muscular legs, massive tails and razor-sharp teeth. They eat smaller members of their own kind and occasionally attack and kill human beings. They mainly feed on carrion. Historians believe the mythological Chinese dragon may have been fashioned after the creature whose long, forked, blazing orange tongue seemed to resemble fire. Komodo dragons can live to be 100 years old.

The first people in Indonesia were dark-skinned woolly-haired pygmy Negritos who arrived in Indonesia about 30,000 to 40,000 years ago. Australoids with dark skin and wooly hair, had broad flat noses and pronounced brow ridges. Between 3,000 and 500 B.C. both these groups were driven into the highlands and jungles by the migration of Mongoloid peoples from the northern Indochina region: the Proto-Malaya and the Deutro-Malays.

The Proto-Malays, represented today by ethnic groups such as the Bataks and Dayaks, brought with them a Neolithic or New Stone Age technology. They lived in village settlements, domesticated animals and cultivated crops. Remnants of their culture can be seen today in the megaliths found in Sumatra. Their descendants constitute the majority of Indonesia's ethnically diverse population.

The Hindu and Buddhist religions have made a difference in Indonesia. In the first to fifth centuries A.D. the Indonesians started to "Indianize" their own kingdoms. They invited Brahman scholars to their own courts and sent students to study in India. They learned about astronomy and navigational techniques, figure sculpturing and textile dyeing and they adopted numerous Sanskrit words. They introduced spices such as cardamom and turmeric into their food as well as acquiring domesticated horses and elephants and they adopted new architectural styles.

India's twin religions—Hinduism and Buddhism---began a peaceful coexistence in Java and Sumatra. Over a period of 1,000 years Indonesia's history is that of the rise and fall of many Hindu and Buddhist kingdoms. By about the eighth century, there were two kingdoms: the Buddhist Srivijaya kingdom in Sumatra, which ruled the seas and major marine routes for the next 600 years and the Hindu-Buddhist Mataram and Sailendra kingdoms of central Java, which controlled inland rice production for a shorter period of time. Sumatra was called Swarna Dwipa or "Gold Island". Java was called Yava Dwipa or "Rice Island." The Srivijava Kingdom was based on foreign trade and controlled the strategic Strait of Malacca. From there spices, incense and other rare goods were traded between China and India.

The Javanese Mataram and Sailendra kingdoms were more spiritually orientated. The rich soils and wet rice agriculture supported a huge population which was later employed for the building of the magnificent Borobudur and Prombanan temples. Eventually, there emerged a powerful new Hindu kingdom in Java called the Majapahit established in 1294 in an area known for its pabit meaning bitter, maja fruit. This empire marked the golden age of Indonesian history.

The Majapahit Empire united the whole of Indonesia and parts of the Malay Peninsula and ruled for two centuries. A true Indonesian identity emerged and a unique Javanese art and culture developed and flourished. Around the 14th Century this great kingdom went into decline and was invaded by the new Islamic state of Demak. The entire Hindu-Javanese aristocracy fled to Bali leaving a rich Indian Indonesian heritage. Even Marco Polo, who visited Indonesia in1292 noted that Islam was already established in parts of Aceh in north Sumatra. From Aceh, Islam spread to the rest of Indonesia along the trade routes and the paths of economic expansion. People were converted in the process.

By the 15th and 16th centuries many Indonesian rulers had made Islam the state religion to strengthen ties with the neighboring port of Malacca, which had then become the center of Islam and trade. The growing international Islamic trade network brought more power and wealth.

The Portuguese came to Indonesia in 1509 and established trading posts. Their profits encouraged other European traders to come to the region. While the English explored the Malayan peninsula and the Spanish in the Philippines, the Dutch arrived in Indonesia. In 1596, four Dutch ships arrived at Ban ten in Maluku. The Dutch brought back spices to Holland. More Dutch ships arrived over the next 10 years. The Dutch took more spices back to Holland. The Dutch established a strong foothold in Jayakarta (modern Jakarta) which they renamed Batavia. They gained control of the clove producing Celebes Island known as Sulawesi today.

In 1949 Indonesia became independent from the Dutch. There were 169 political parties struggling for power. In 1959 Sukarno declared martial law and established his policy of "Guided Democracy." Sukarno revised Indonesia's foreign policy. Within Indonesia the entire civil service was reorganized. The economy gradually set out on a path of high growth through sensible policies aimed at controlling foreign investments, expanding oil exports, slowing population growth and increasing food and production.

Bali, Java and North Sumatra currently draw the most tourists. The government is encouraging the growth of the tourism industry by restoring ancient monuments such as Borobudur; by constructing new hotels, theaters and art galleries in cultural centers such as Yogyarkarta and by promoting an airstrip at Jona Jaraja. New hotels, restaurants, bars and souvenir shops along seafronts are currently available for tourists to enjoy. Indonesia is a charming place to visit.

THREE

Gardening Techniques

Rose gardens exist all over the world. Many people grow a variety of roses in their gardens. There are white, yellow, red and pink roses. Rose bushes are filled with beautiful roses. Rose bushes can be planted near fences and driveways. Roses need to be carefully cultivated with rich soil. They should be watered regularly. Weeds need to be removed around roses.

Garden soil needs to be enriched with quality soil. Good soil can be pressed into clay. Sandy soil is not rich. Mulch helps to stop weeds from growing and spreading in your garden. Mulch holds soil in the ground. On windy days the soil is protected under the mulch.

Irrigation is important in your garden. Trenches should be dug around bushes, trees and newly planted flowers so water will remain close to these plants. Gardens should be watered at least once a week. Some new plants may need to be watered more than other plants.

Organize your flowers in multi-colors. Be sure to select a wide variety of flowers and shrubs to cultivate an interesting garden.

Be sure to leave enough room between each plant so each plant will grow well. Don't let the water drain off. Water shouldn't be wasted. Rain water should be able to absorb the roots of all your garden plants because of proper irrigation.

Take care of your garden by constant weeding, regular watering and careful trimming. The more you look after your garden the better it will look. Raking fallen weeds and leaves away is also important in the upkeep of your garden. Enjoy gardening!

FOUR

Mountain Climbing

Mountain climbing is a challenging experience. Each mountain is slightly different to climb. However, a mountain climber learns from experience how to climb up steep ledges and slopes until he or she reaches the top of the mountain.

Mountain climbing equipment is necessary in order to climb safely: Ropes, rock hooks, hammers, climbing boots, tents, wooden stacks, canvas coverings, packed food, ice containers for meat and dairy products, back packs and mountain clothes. It is essential to bring necessary climbing equipment in order to succeed in mountain climbing.

Mountain climbers should have plenty of rest before planning to climb any mountain. Climbing boots with hooks help make it easier to climb up slopes. Ropes are used to hold mountain climbers as they go up high, dangerous slopes to ledges. Dark glasses are usually worn to protect one from glaring Sunlight. Gloves keep your hands warm in the colder, mountain climate.

It is important to know how to set up tents properly on mountain ledges and plateaus. Wooden sticks should be hammered into the ledge. Then the tent canvases should be pulled up by ropes until they are standing. Canvas should be placed on the tent floors. Bedrolls are spread out in each tent. Each tent should be at least six feet apart or more in order to have enough space for privacy.

Flashlights and kerosene lamps are needed when it gets dark at night. Campfires may not always be available on high snowy ledges. Mountain climbers need to bundle up to keep warm. Thick fur coats help to keep them warmer especially at night. Sometimes campfires can be lit if there is a place to dig a hole. Twigs and branches are piled up in the campfire hole. Then the twigs are lit. When the fire spreads to the branches the fire begins to blaze. When the campfire is blazing the mountain climbers can feel the warmth readily from the campfire.

Mountain climbers need to prepare their food carefully. Meat id unpacked and prepared over the campfire such as hamburger, chicken and fish. Even hot dogs can easily be prepared. Beans are warmed up to eat. Cut vegetables and some fruit are prepared to eat. Hot coffee and hot chocolate are prepared to drink. It is important to eat enough food in order to have enough energy to climb better.

Climate changes during the day and night on mountains. It may be warm and Sunny for awhile. Then, suddenly it begins to rain. The rain may be very cold. Snow may fall at any time. Climbers should wear hoods in order to protect their heads. When it is warm jackets and coats should be taken off. It is not good to get too warm. Sweating should be avoided. Hyperthermia should be avoided. In fact, if hyperthermia takes place a climber needs special treatment. Pneumonia can occur if a victim experiences hyperthermia.

Experienced mountain climbers know how to use mountain climbing equipment. They have learned to climb difficult, steep slopes. They hook their shoes into rock crevasses as they climb higher and higher. They use ropes to pull themselves up to each ledge. Slope by slope experienced climbers are able to climb to the top of the mountain.

Once mountain climbers reach the top of the highest slope they have reached the summit. They can enjoy a fabulous view of the valleys below. Many panoramic views are spectacular to view. There are many vivid colors in the sky and valleys. It is a victory to reach the top of a mountain. Climbing back down a mountain is challenging. Climbers must carefully place their feet in rock crevasses and cracks step by step using ropes, metal hooks and spiked shoes.

Mountain climbers must keep in good shape and maintain excellent health in order to climb mountains. Each mountain expedition should be well planned with the best mountain climbing supplies. Cameras should be brought to film different scenes and views.

Mountain climbers should read about mountain climbers. They usually join mountain climbing organizations where they meet other mountain climbers. Mountain climbing can be worthwhile as well as challenging.

FIVE

The Avalanche

An avalanche can occur suddenly because of loud sounds, excessive rain and earthquakes. A sudden crashing of rocks tumble down and a mountainside comes sliding down to the valley below. An avalanche is usually very dangerous. It can damage people, animals, plants and houses once the debris falls below on to objects on the ground.

Iris Camden lived near a mountain in a charming cabin in a wooded location. She was surrounded by evergreen trees. Wild animals roamed in the woods. Deer, rabbits, squirrels, red foxes and raccoons dwelled in the woods.

The log cabin Iris lived in was fairly spacious. The Sun beamed into the cabin through the different, framed windows. Iris enjoyed living in the cozy cabin. She put logs in the fireplace and created a fire in her fireplace. The burning embers kept her cabin warm day and night. The fireplace also lit up the cabin.

Iris went walking in the woods to be close to nature. She observed squirrels scurry up and down the evergreen trees. Rabbits were nibbling wild flowers and grass. A few deer were eating leaves and ferns in the woods. Iris continued walking in the woods. She finally sat down under a large evergreen tree to rest. She felt at peace in the woods. The Sun gleamed through the trees. She felt the warmth from the rays of the Sun.

The weather was pleasant during the summer and early autumn. Iris went swimming and boating. She played tennis and golf with her friends during weekends and holidays. She worked in a chemistry laboratory as a chemist during the week days. Her life was going smoothly.

When winter approached it began to rain. It continued to rain for days and days. A lot of rain came down and began to flood the region where Iris lived. One night an avalanche suddenly took place when the nearby mountainside quickly slid down into the valley below and into the woods. The avalanche crashed into Iris's cabin during the night while she was sleeping in bed. She was not warned in advance so she was trapped in her cabin because rocks and mountain debris had landed all around and on top of her cabin. Windows were broken.

Iris woke up in shock when she heard the loud crashing sound. She got up and tried to open her front door. The door wouldn't open because it was stuck with mud, rocks and mountain debris. Iris wasn't able to go out of any windows or doors. She realized that she was trapped in her cabin.

Iris began to feel panicky because she was trapped in her cabin. She tried to think about what to do. She decided to call 911 on her cell phone because her regular phone did not work because the telephone wires had been damaged. She was able to reach 911. She told the person who answered the phone that she was trapped in her cabin. She described her location.

An emergency ambulance was sent to Iris's cabin. The ambulance attendants struggled to clear the mountain debris from Iris's cabin door. It took hours to clear the rocks, mud and debris around the cabin entrance. A special bulldozer was brought in to clear the avalanche debris, rocks and mud.

Finally, the avalanche debris, rocks and mud was removed. The front door was torn down. The ambulance attendants entered the cabin and found Iris, who had been waiting for hours to be rescued. She had experienced stress, anxiety and fear. She was in a state of severe shock. The ambulance attendants put Iris in a cot and covered her with a blanket. They carried her out of the cabin in the stretcher to their ambulance.

Iris was taken to the nearest hospital to the emergency ward. A doctor examined Iris carefully. Fortunately, she didn't have any broken bones. A nurse calmed Iris down by sedating her. She became very sleepy and she fell asleep from the sedation. She woke up the next day. She was hungry and concerned about what had happened to her. She knew she was in the hospital.

Iris thought about the avalanche that damaged her cabin. After several hours Iris was released from the hospital. She called one of her best friends to come pick her up at the hospital. When the friend arrived at the hospital Iris told her what had happened to her. Iris stayed at her friend's home until she could find another place to live. Iris missed her cabin in the woods. It had been completely damaged and it had to be torn down.

Iris finally found another house to live in. She lived in town near her job. She felt safer there. However, the life she had lived in her cabin was special. She missed walking in the woods. She hoped there would never be another avalanche.

SIX

Skiing Competition

Skiing is a popular sport. Many people learn to ski. Children as well as adults learn to ski. Skiing equipment is needed. Skis are needed and sports clothes are worn when a person skis.

Jeromy Wilkins, who lived near Sun Valley in California, learned to ski at the age of 10. He became a skillful skier by the time he was 15 years old. Jeromy entered skiing competitions. He won several skiing awards.

Jeromy became a top skier. He decided to go to Insbrook in Austria to ski at the International Skiing Olympics. He entered the skiing contest. There were thirty skiers who entered the skiing Olympics.

Accommodations were booked in advance in Innsbruck. So, when Jeromy arrived in Insbrook he was able to go to his hotel immediately. A hotel room was available because it had been reserved for him. Jeromy paid the hotel bill in advance for three nights and four days. His hotel room was located in the 7th floor. He had a spectacular view of the skiing area from his hotel room.

Hanging plants were in the balcony windows. The air was crisp and fresh.

The Olympic contest was held the next day. Jeremy had gone to bed at 10 p.m. He got up at 7 a.m. to have breakfast first. He ate breakfast downstairs in the Austrian Coffee Shop. He ate a hearty breakfast consisting of scrambled eggs, Austrian bacon and ham plus delicious 7 grain pancakes. He drank orange juice and later had some hot coffee. Jeromy felt full after breakfast.

Insbrook is a scenic mountain city in Austria. Jeromy walked around the mountain streets of this charming city. He browsed at shop windows. As he strolled down the streets he came to a clock shop. He walked into this shop. Hundreds of clocks were displayed around this shop in shelves and on counters and tables. Many of these clocks had been made in Switzerland and Germany. Many of them were ticking with miniature people or birds moving in and out of the clocks. Jeromy decided to buy a chalet clock to bring back to his home in America in Sun Valley, California.

The time went by. Jeromy had to be at the ski Olympics Competition by 10:30 a.m. The competition would begin at 11:00 a.m. He went back to his hotel and dressed in his skiing outfit. He wore a warm cap and a red woolen lined jacket over a turtleneck, warm woolen sweater and warm pants plus ski boots. He picked up his skis and headed toward the Olympics location on a famous skiing slope.

Many people were at the skiing slope. Thirty competitors were arriving for the Olympic Competition. Jeromy lined up to prepare for the race. He put on his skis and he was ready for the race. When his name was called and a whistle was blown, Jeromy mounted at the top of the high slope. He began skiing down the steep slope. He was very skillful and he skied with grace and confidence. He was used to skiing back home in Sun Valley. Other skiers were in front and back of him. He continued skiing swiftly down the long slope past trees covered with snow.

Jeromy landed at the bottom of the high, narrow slope. He had to lift his skis several times over rocks and slumpy snow to avoid falling. He had managed to ski very quickly with agility for five miles. He came to the final location and stopped after controlling his skis. Other skiers also stopped nearby. Jeromy waited to find out who had won.

The Olympics Sponsor finally announced the winners after all thirty skiers had arrived at the end of the competition. Jeromy was anxious to find out if he had won. He had attended many skiing competitions. He had lost many of them or came in third or fourth.

Today was another day to attempt to win a skiing competition. The judge finally announced the winner. The skiing judge said, "Jack Jones came in third. Shirley Smith came in second." Then there was a pause. Finally the judge announced the first place winner. He said, "First place goes to Jeromy Wilkins from California."

Jeromy was very excited. He walked over to the judge. The Olympics judge said, "Congratulations Jeromy!" He handed Jeromy a beautiful gold trophy and a check of $10,000. Jeromy was overjoyed to receive the gold cup and large sum of money. He said, "Thank you."

When Jeromy went back to Sun Valley, California with his trophy and money he showed his parents, relatives and friends his trophy. He continued to ski. He met other skiers and he continued to participate in more skiing competitions.

— SEVEN —

Telephone Friends

People who live miles away from one another depend on the use of their telephone. They call one another to visit on the phone. They may never see one another in person for many years. Being telephone friends is the next best way to visit and to keep in touch with one another.

My friend Adrianne Stillman and I seldom see each other in person. She lives miles away from me. She has a busy daily schedule. Carole works odd hours on her one to one teaching assignments. Adrianne calls me after she gets home at 9:00 p.m. She needs to express herself to me about her problems, challenges and teaching experiences.

Adrianne needs a "sounding board" to express her feelings. She doesn't watch television. She lives in a big house by herself. Her children are grown up and have moved away. Adrianne is isolated from neighbors, who live far away from her in the country. Adrianne often talks about her boyfriend who lives 40 miles away from her. She has been going with him for 15 years. She has decided not to marry him.

Often Adrianne calls me at odd hours to express her strong feelings about her boyfriend. She complains about him because she claims he is too demanding. He comes to her house and eats her food. Finally, he took her out to eat at a restaurant from time to time. Adrianne complained to me that she spent too much for food when her boyfriend, Alex stayed with her.

Adrianne taught students on a one to one basis. Each student came to a small room where Adrianne instructed them. She did not receive a large annual salary. She had to economize every day in order to have enough money to pay her bills.

Adrianne's boyfriend is well off with a good retirement, Social Security and savings. He owns a three story elegant home in Morrow Bay overlooking the scenic bay. Adrianne drives over to his house and stays overnight for several days at a time when she had time off on the weekend.

Alex invited Adrianne to travel with him to the Middle East. He has relatives in Egypt where he grew up. He had to come to America in his late twenties to teach Mathematics. He taught Math at the university level for over 32 years. He retired at age 60. Alex had a lot of time to himself after he retired. He didn't like to live alone in his three story house.

However, Adrianne told Alex that she preferred to live in her own house up in the hills. Alex hoped she would change her mind and that she would come live with him. Adrianne continued to live in her own house.

Alex tried to get along with Adrianne's two children who were already grown up. For some reason Alex wasn't able to get along with them. Adrianne had been married 26 years and was now divorced. She had left her first husband because he was difficult to live with.

Adrianne told me all about her marriage and the problems she had with her first husband Perry. She never went back together with him once they separated. Adrianne has been very hesitant to get married again after what she experienced in her first marriage. She preferred to be on her own. She complained about her first husband Perry as well as Alex.

I have a number of telephone friends who I seldom see in person. They are too busy and they have unusual time schedules. We talk on the phone about our feelings, lifestyles, interests and personal problems when we call each other.

EIGHT

Creative Endeavors

We can pursue creative endeavors. Artistic abilities can be expressed such as drawing, painting, sculptures, pottery and various crafts such as woodwork, weaving and carvings. Musical talents can be cultivated such as singing, vocal solos, playing the piano, organ, harp, clarinet, violin, viola, cello, oboe, trumpet, saxophone, chimes, drums and cymbals.

You can become a writer of poetry, novels, nonfiction and plays. Learning to write is a valuable experience. Learning to express yourself effectively is useful. You can express your deepest thoughts and feelings on paper. Your ideas and opinions can become permanent writings. It is exciting to have writings published.

So, be a creative person by developing your abilities and talents.

NINE

Learn About Bees

Bees are becoming extinct. Perhaps pollution is causing their disappearance. Bees live in hives created by worker bees. The hive is carefully woven together step by step.

Hundreds of bees live in a hive. They produce wax cells to put nectar in which produces honey. Bees live on honey. The queen bee is protected and fed by worker bees. The queen bee is fertilized by drones which are male bees. Once they fertilize the queen bee they die. They have served their purpose.

Bees live in forests high up in trees in their hives. Bears are able to knock bee hives down to the ground. Bears eat up the honey in a hive. The bees must build another hive. The queen bee is put in the new hive.

Tribes in forests and jungles have discovered honey when tribesmen climb trees to knock down bee hives. These tribesmen gathered the honeycombs out of the hive. So, again, honey was taken away from the bees.

Some people create bee hives in boxes with vent holes. Bees can come in and out of the manmade beehives to hunt for pollen in flowers. These bees produce honey. More bees are produced by the queen bee who lays many bee eggs that eventually hatch into worker bees, drones and more queen bees.

Honey is nutritious as well as delicious. We enjoy putting honey on waffles, pancakes and toast. Honey helps us stay healthy. We need to protect bees by protecting their hives. If honeycombs are removed from hives enough honeycombs should be left in bee hives so bees will have enough honey to eat. We should avoid causing pollution so bees will survive.

TEN

Why People Gossip

Why do people gossip about other people? Individuals usually gossip about people they do not like and who they resent or hate. By gossiping a person releases negative feelings and frustrations about those people they feel negative reactions about. Gossip is a form of breaking the Golden Rule. Negative feelings cause the listeners to gossip to respond to in a negative manner toward the person or people gossiped about.

Ellen Martin was a very verbal person. She lived in a small town known as Los Gatos in California. She was sensitive and had developed a strong reaction to certain people she knew. Ellen worked in a clerical department at a local business establishment. She sat at a desk in a small cubicle walled in. Other clerical workers sat in their small cubicles. Each cubicle had an opening so employees who walked by could see other employees at their desks.

The business office opened at 8:00 a.m. and closed at 5:00 p.m. Ellen and other office employees were expected to be at work on time. Ellen had clerical work to do at her desk. She typed invoices, letters and also did some bookkeeping. She was an efficient worker.

During coffee breaks and lunch time she left her small office to go relax and have a cup of coffee and to eat a snack and to eat lunch. Ellen had become familiar with other employees. She often walked into the employee's lounge to have her coffee break. Coffee break lasted 20 minutes.

Ellen had ample time to chat with other employees. She heard them talk about daily news, personal problems and office work. Some employees often gossiped about their personal lives. They spoke about their family life, hobbies and interests.

Ellen expressed her feelings and opinions about her life. She was able to unwind by gossiping about her concerns and frustrations. Ellen spoke to Darlene, Sherry and Alice who she knew for some time. Ellen had been working at the business firm for three years. Her annual salary was $20,000. She had started at $17,700 when she began this job as a clerical worker several years ago.

Ellen sat in the lounge room near her employee friends. She unwound by gossiping about her mother who was handicapped while she sat at a couch near Darlene, Sherry and Alice. Ellen said, "My mother expects me to come over after work to clean her house and make her dinner! I wish I could go back to my apartment after work to rest. I didn't sleep well last night." Darlene, who had been listening while she sipped her coffee, replied, "Why doesn't your mother hire a housekeeper and cook?" Ellen answered, "She can't afford to hire anyone. She is living on a small pension."

Sherry and Alice were sitting nearby. Sherry spoke, "My mother lives with me. She can't afford a place of her own. She is a "noose" around my neck. My boyfriend feels awkward around her when he comes over. We don't have any privacy! If we get married he doesn't want my mother to live with us." Ellen, Darlene and Alice were listening to Sherry as they sipped their coffee and munched some corn chips and cookies.

Alice looked concerned. She said," My mother passed away a year ago. I miss her. She died in the hospital after she suffered a heart attack. I wish she was still living." Ellen replied, "Did you have to clean her house?" Alice looked upset. She answered, "No. But if my mother needed my help I would have cleaned her house." Ellen thought about what Alice had just said.

Coffee break time was over. Ellen, Sherry, Alice and Darlene went back to their small cubicles to continue working. Ellen received a phone call from the office manager. when she was working at her desk. The office manager said, "Ellen, I want you to work overtime today. We have an important clerical report to finish before the deadline." Ellen was frustrated because she had responsibilities at home after work. However, she knew her boss expected her to work overtime. So, Ellen replied, "I will work overtime." The office manager answered, "Good. Come to my office to pick up the clerical work." Ellen replied, "O.K. I'll be there right away." She hung up the phone.

Ellen knew her mother needed her. Yet, her job came first. She called her mother immediately and told her that she had to work overtime. Ellen's mother was disappointed. She said, "I need you here Ellen. I can't cook dinner. My house is a mess!"

Ellen answered, "I have to work overtime to keep my job! Can you ask Bernice to fix your dinner and clean your house?"

Ellen's mother replied on the phone, "Bernice is out of town. I don't have anyone else to help me." Ellen pondered and thought about her mother's situation. She said, "I'll order you some food to be delivered at your house. What would you like for dinner?" Ellen's mother answered, "I'll have Chinese food. Order me Almond Chicken Chop Suey, rice, egg fu yong and shrimp." Ellen wrote down her mother's request. She told her mother that the Chinese food would be delivered at 5:30 p.m.

Ellen hung up and quickly called a Chinese restaurant after looking up the phone number in a telephone directory. She ordered the Chinese food her mother requested. Then, Ellen walked over to the office manager's office to pick up the clerical work. The office manager handed her a large file of clerical information to work on. It looked like a lot of work. However, Ellen didn't complain. She accepted the work and took it back to her small office. She knew it would take time to complete this extra work. She was already tired by 3 p.m. from her regular work load.

Afternoon coffee break was at 3 p.m. to 3:20 p.m. Ellen decided to take her break as usual. She needed to relax and unwind for at least twenty minutes. She walked into the employees lounge and poured herself some hot coffee to sip. She sat down on a lounge couch.

Alice, Darlene and Sherry were already sipping coffee in the lounge. Ellen looked at them with a tired expression. Darlene said, "Ellen, are you alright?" Ellen replied, "I'm exhausted! I am going to have to work overtime today. I have a big clerical file to work on! I probably won't get out of the office until late tonight!" Alice asked, "What about your mother? I thought you were going over to her place to fix dinner and clean her house?" Ellen responded, "I have to work over time because the office manager asked me

to stay to finish the clerical project. I have ordered Chinese food to be delivered to my mother's house. The mess in her house will have to be cleaned another day."

Sherry, Darlene and Alice looked at Ellen with sympathy. They knew Ellen was tired. Now, she had to work overtime. They decided not to gossip about the office manager. If any gossip got back to her they might lose their jobs. They needed to work to earn a living. So, they said nothing about the office manager.

Ellen and her office associates went back to work after coffee break. Sherry, Darlene and Alice went home promptly at 5:00 p.m. Ellen remained in the office to work on the extra clerical work. She worked until 9:30 p.m. in order to complete the clerical work. The next day was Friday. She would bring the completed clerical work to the office manager's office.

Ellen was quite weary at 9:30 p.m. She had ordered a tuna sandwich with potato salad and ice tea to be delivered to her office for dinner which she ate at 6:00 p.m. After Ellen left the office, once she locked up, she headed to her apartment to rest and hopefully recuperate from the long day's work. The next morning she returned to work at 8:00 a.m. She still felt tired from the previous day's work.

The clerical work was taken to the office manager's office. The office manager smiled as she received the completed work. She said, "Thanks Ellen for working overtime. You will receive double time for the extra time that you worked." Ellen felt better. Her boss had appreciated that she had worked overtime. She was glad to receive more money to pay her expenses.

Ellen went back to her office and she called her mother. She asked her mother if she had received the Chinese food the night before. Her mother told Ellen that the Chinese dinner had been delivered. She said the Chinese food was very delicious. Ellen's mother asked," When are you coming over to see me?" Ellen replied, "I'll be over after work today. I'll take you out to dinner. Be ready at 5:30 p.m." Ellen's mother was pleased that Ellen planned to take her out.

At office break Ellen told her office associates she planned to take her mother out to a nice restaurant after work. They smiled and realized that Ellen was going to do something thoughtful for her mother.

ELEVEN

Joyous Living

Joyous living is a very uplifting experience. Enthusiasm in daily living helps us feel positive feelings about living. Joyous moments make up for moments when we feel sad and despondent. The joy of being One infinite reality transforms us and awakens us to a higher calling.

Higher consciousness helps a soul increase his or her vitality and light. Higher vibrations can manifest when we experience joyous living. Each day should be lived to the fullest. Every minute counts. We need to appreciate God and live with gratitude and appreciation in our hearts.

Joyous living should be a continuous, ongoing experience. When we enjoy Sunbeams on leaves and flowers and we smell the fresh fragrances of nature we become close to God's creations. Experience climbing a mountain slope. Once you reach the mountaintop you can look at verdant valleys below. Panoramic visions are spectacular to view. Sparkling oceans and rippling, diamond light dazzles us. Rainbows emanate bright colors of yellow, red, purple, green and orange.

We have much to appreciate especially when we enjoy sunrises and brilliant sunsets, mists on a colorful meadow and azure blue skies with cloud patterns spreading everywhere across the sky. Star beams dazzle our eyes at night. We can enjoy the wind, sea currents and warmth of the Sun. Joyous living is a wondrous experience.

TWELVE

Ways To Prepare Eggs

There are a variety of ways to prepare eggs. Eggs can be boiled to chop up and sprinkle with herbs. Boiled eggs can be painted for Easter egg hunts. Eggs can be scrambled and cheese, bacon and ham can be added to these eggs. Eggs can be fried over easy. Eggs Benedict are poplar on sourdough muffins with ham.

Deviled eggs take careful preparation. First, the eggs must be boiled. When the eggs are boiled the yellow part is removed and mixed with spices and cut pickles or sliced olives. The whites of eggs are cut in halves. The yellow mixture is stuffed in hollow openings in the egg whites. Deviled eggs are placed on trays or plates as finger food at parties, potlucks and picnics. Deviled eggs are served at special dinners.

Eggs are made into a variety of omelets. These are ham and cheese omelet's, Denver omelet's, vegetarian omelet's with cut vegetables such as tomatoes, olives, green peppers, mushrooms, squash and cheese. Chili bean omelet's are also eaten.

Eggs are used in cake dough, waffles, pancakes and cookies. Egg whites are used in lemon chiffon pies and baked Alaska. Eggs help blend flour and sugar in dough.

Eggs have been eaten for thousands of years. Chinese people eat eggs that have fermented for years. Eggs are eaten by millions of people. Eggs continue to be prepared on a daily basis in many ways.

THIRTEEN

Breathing Incense

Incense has been used in churches, meditation rooms, temples, Ashrams and people's homes. Cedar, sage, rose, jasmine and frankincense are often burned in incense burners.

Why are people breathing the fragrance of incense? Because incense may have a healing effect. Incense may cleanse you and rejuvenate you. The pleasant scents from incense may relax you.

Hindus burn fragrant incense on altars in their temples. The incense permeates the temple relaxing those who attend the temples. Ancient civilizations such as Babylonians, Sumerians and Egyptians burned incense. This custom has been passed from one civilization to the next civilization.

Breathing incense has a magnetic effect on the human nervous system. Many people around the world burn incense in their homes, shops and religious groups. Incense may remain a popular custom around the world.

FOURTEEN

Whistling

Whistling is a form of self expression with a blowing sound. Many people have learned to whistle. Each person makes a different whistling sound because of the size and shape of their mouth. Each whistling sound is unique.

In Switzerland, Swiss yodelers make loud whistling sounds as well as yodeling sounds. They echo across the Swiss Alps with their sounds. Whistling is a form of communication.

Some entertainers know how to whistle quite well. They create melodies which are very musical. Professional whistlers entertain large audiences at County Fairs, Circuses and talent shows. Some whistlers are able to make two whistling sounds at once.

Whistlers can perform with other background instruments. Whistlers can blend in with other whistlers as well as other musical instruments. Some whistlers make a living by entertaining audiences at Melodrama theaters and on public stages.

People will go on whistling for fun and to entertain other people. They learn to whistle in different ways to attract the attention of other people. Whistlers round their lips and blow air through their rounded lips to create whistling sounds.

FIFTEEN

Cafeteria Experience

Food is served at school cafeterias from elementary school, high school and college. The food may be served directly at breakfast, lunch and dinner. At elementary school and high school cafeterias specific daily menus are followed. Hot dogs, coleslaw, jello and milk may be served in elementary school cafeterias.

Elementary school children pick up their breakfast and lunch at a food serving section. They carry a tray of food to cafeteria tables. Children sit together and eat their lunches. They have an opportunity to visit while they eat. Eggs, toast and waffles with milk may be served at breakfast. Cereal with milk may be added to the breakfast meal.

Other menus at elementary schools and high schools may be steaks, fries, green salad with milk and cobbler; macaroni and cheese, cold slaw, milk and cake; hamburger patties, mashed potatoes, green salad, milk and ice-cream; fish and fries, cold slaw, milk and cookies may be another meal. Spaghetti and meatballs, green salad, milk and jello; hash made with sliced, diced potatoes and beef or ham, cold slaw, milk and cobbler are different meals served at lunch. Dinner is not served at elementary school because elementary school children go home at 3:00 p.m. They are not at school in the evenings. High school students go home in the afternoon as well. So, they do not eat dinner at the school cafeteria.

College cafeterias serve breakfast, lunch and dinner. There is more variety of hot dishes, salads, desserts and drinks. A wide selection of foods is served every day. College students select different foods and sit together in small groups or by themselves. Two college students may sit together and visit while they eat. College cafeterias are usually open all day so college students can select food throughout the day and in the evenings to 8:00 p.m. or 9:00 p.m. because there are night classes and extension courses.

College cafeterias are places for social opportunities. Many college students go to college cafeterias to eat and socialize between their classes. Students can relax and meet other people in college cafeterias. New friendships may take place because of social contacts in college cafeterias.

Public cafeterias downtown in big cities are buffet styles. There is a wide selection of food. People select the food they want. They pay the cashier who adds up the cost of each tray of food. Certain people sit together and socialize while they eat their selected meal. Cafeteria food is prepared in advance so that it is ready when customers come into the cafeteria to eat. Cafeteria food generally is less expensive than restaurant food.

There are cafeterias in large museums, shopping malls and plazas. Many people enjoy eating at cafeterias because the food is ready to serve.

SIXTEEN

Driving A Car

At the age of 16, teenagers learn to drive a car. Parents and older brothers and sisters teach younger sisters and brothers to drive a car. It is important to learn how to drive. We depend on cars so we can go places readily.

A driver should learn all the rules and expectations about driving a car. A driver should sit correctly behind the steering wheel. He or she should turn on the motor first. Drivers should know how to change the gear shift. The gear shift has P for parking. R means reverse. D1 D2 D3 D4 means drive. N is neutral. N is after reverse. Drive shifts are after N (neutral).

Every driver must learn to change gears immediately in order to drive properly. Drivers must know where the brakes and clutch are located below the steering wheel near his feet. The brakes are on the left. The clutch is on the right. Drivers must use the gas pedal to cause the car to move. The more the driver presses the gas pedal the faster the car will move. If a driver releases his right foot from the gas pedal his or her car will slow down and eventually stop. Brakes are used to stop a car. The brake is pulled to maintain the car in a motionless position.

Speed limits should be observed on streets, freeways and avenues. Generally cars may travel at 65 miles per hour on freeways. Trucks and large vehicles are expected to go 55 miles an hour on freeways. In town drivers are expected to go 35 miles an hour. Near schools and railroads the speed limit is 25 miles an hour.

Traffic lights must be observed. Yellow means to yield and prepare to stop. Green means to go. Railroad signs indicate railroad crossings. Deer signs warn drivers that deer might be in the area. Double yellow-orange lines mean not to pass over the line on both sides of the road. If a dotted line exists a driveway may pass over the dotted line to go around cars in front of this driver's car.

Intersections exist. Drivers should turn right correctly in the far right lane if the driver is in the right lane. If the driver is in the center lane he or she should remain in the center lane. Cars in the left lane should turn left at the intersection.

Good drivers observe the speed limit and all traffic signs and other signs. They are careful on freeways, streets and roads when they are driving. They are careful at all times to avoid accidents. They take care of their cars and renew their driver's licenses. They maintain car insurance and they carry the up-to-date car registration and insurance information in their cars. They respect traffic laws and obey them.

SEVENTEEN

Outdoor Theater

Outdoor theaters exist especially in warm climates where there is little rain. Outdoor theaters exist in England, Spain, Portugal, France, Italy and America. The Greeks and Romans performed plays in outdoor arenas. Romans and Greeks sat on high rise, stone seats to watch dramas and musicals.

In Rome there are amphitheaters which are outdoors. Amphitheaters exist in other Roman cities and villages such as Milan, Milos, Venice and Naples. In Greece amphitheaters exist in Athens and the Island of Capri. In France, outdoor theaters and puppet shows are performed in Paris, Brittany and the French Riviera. In England, outdoor theaters exist in London, Cornwall and other places. In Spain, outdoor theaters exist in Madrid and Seville. Portugal is known for outdoor theaters where Flamenco dancing and Portuguese music are also performed in Lisbon and Barcelona.

Outdoor theaters existed in ancient civilizations such as Sumeria, Egypt and Babylonia. Self expression has taken place by acting out dramas and music. Creative expression is a way to communicate many feelings and make believe desires and actions on stages. Humanity has always expressed illusionary dramas as imitations of life.

In America, outdoor theaters exist in Solvang, California, Carmel and Monterey, California and in Hollywood, California at the Hollywood Bowl. Outdoor theaters provide benches and outdoor seats for audiences. The weather may change. Outdoor performances are usually performed during warmer months in the year. Outdoor theaters also exist in the islands of Hawaii.

Solvang, California and Carmel, California are well known for outdoor theaters for many years. Dramas and musicals will go on being performed outdoors at outdoor theaters.

EIGHTEEN

Director Of Stage Plays And Screenplays

A director of stage plays and screenplays is in charge of actors and actresses. The director directs the actors and actresses. He or she instructs them how to say their lines and how to move on stage. An effective director knows how to instruct everyone on stage how to act and respond step by step during each act in a stage play.

Screenplays have much shorter scenes in a film. There are hundreds of scenes spliced together to create a film. Many scenes are less than a minute. The dialogue lines can be seen away from the camera. Actors and actresses can look at the lines as they perform on the set. They don't have to memorize their lines.

There is no audience observing what happens on movie sets. The director can stop the dialogue at anytime and have the actors and actresses practicing their dialogue and set movements. The director can give directions to the cameramen as well. Close up shots are important. Main actors and actresses are focused on during filming.

Lighting is very important because scenes must be seen in the film. If there are too many shadows, the film will not turn out good. The director may notice if there isn't enough light on the set. His or her directing role is vital so the film will be well presented.

So, acting, props and sets and lighting effect the quality of the film. The director makes a big difference in how a stage play and screenplay are presented. The director strives to produce an excellent stage play and screenplay.

NINTEEN

Making Props And Sets

Props and sets are important for the production of stage plays and screenplays. Realistic sets are carefully planned. Props are movable objects used on each set. For example, the set may be a living room. The props are furniture, paintings on the wall. Furniture can be moved on an off of the set.

Elaborate sets are planned with realistic props to create the best effect. Actors and actresses move around in the set using props. An office set has desks, desk chairs, office equipment and office windows. The props are the desks, chairs, typewriters, computers and file cabinets. The actors and actresses sit at the desks in chairs. They may perform at the typewriter or computer. An actor or actress may go to the file cabinet and look for papers in it to act out a scene.

Cowboy scenes are usually in the country in a movie. Props are horses and cattle which move around. Cowboys ride horses on the range. They act out scenes on the range, which are realistic, based on cowboy life.

Sometimes background sets are created in the studio. Trees and rocks and grass props are placed on the set. Actors and actresses stand in the set to act out their roles near the trees, rocks and grassy set which looks real.

Props and sets are needed and are essential so that each scene appears real to produce the illusion of action on the stage or movie set. Many scenes are produced in the studio or on the stage.

TWENTY

Preparing Pastries

Preparing pies, cakes, donuts and tarts take skill in knowing how to bake these pastries. In ancient times pies, cakes, donuts and tarts were not yet discovered. Ancient civilizations ate fresh fruit and nuts for dessert. Sugar had not been discovered in those early days.

Around a thousand years ago Europeans began to prepare pies and tarts for kings and queens. When sugar was processed from sugarcane plants and refined it was finally added to pies, cakes, donuts, tarts and cookies. Wheat was finally refined into flour. Flour, sugar, eggs and milk were mixed together and made into pie dough, cake dough, donut dough and tart dough.

Before sugar was used honey and sweet fruits such as berries, plums, apples and pineapples were used to sweeten pies, cakes and cookies. Vanilla flavor was added to pastries once vanilla beans were brought to Europe and America.

Apple pies are very popular. Apples are cut into chunks and placed in a pie tin which is covered with moist dough made of flour, sugar and eggs. The pie dough is rolled out first and placed in the pie tin and shaped to its glass or tin shape. Cut, fresh apples are sprinkled with cinnamon and other sweeteners such as sugar. The apple pie is baked at 350 degrees for one hour usually until the pie dough is a light brown. The apple pie is cooled off for a period time. The pie is sliced and served in pie plates usually with whipped cream on each piece of pie.

Blackberries, blueberries and strawberries are washed, cut and placed in pie pans after pie dough is formed around the pie pans. A top layer of dough is covered over the berries. Strawberry pie is not baked. However, blueberries and gooseberries are cooked in a pie pan surrounded with pie dough.

Cakes are made of flour, sugar, eggs, salt, baking powder and vanilla seasoning. Chocolate dough is added to chocolate cakes. Whipped cream or frosting is made and spread over the layered cake to add a colorful, tasty frosting covered over the one or two layered cake. Some cakes are a mixture of vanilla and chocolate dough. It is baked in a cake pan in the oven. A swirling effect is designed in the baked cake. The frosting adds to the flavor of the cake.

Fruit tarts are delicious. They are made with fruit and dough. They are much smaller than a regular pie. They may have a tart taste. Donuts are made of flour, eggs sugar and certain baking oils. The dough is shaped into round donuts with holes in the center. Donuts are sprinkled with frosting, candy pieces or sugar.

Pastries are eaten by many people. They buy pies, cakes, donuts, tarts and cookies at bakeries and grocery stores to take home to eat.

—— TWENTY ONE ——

Eucalyptus Trees

Eucalyptus trees have existed on the Earth for millions of years. There are a variety of different types of eucalyptus trees. These ancient trees have grown and spread throughout Australia.

Eucalyptus trees have been brought to America and to parts of Europe. They grow in sandy soil. Eucalyptus leaves have a healing effect. Eucalyptus oil is used for different purposes. Koala Bears eat eucalyptus leaves as the only source of food. They are healthy as they dwell in eucalyptus trees. They depend on eucalyptus leaves in order to survive.

There are many groves of eucalyptus trees especially in California. Eucalyptus trees hold the soil down. Their fragrance is wonderful. California Indians used eucalyptus leaves in their food. Eucalyptus bark was used to build Indian dwellings. Eucalyptus branches were cut into smaller pieces and burned into campfires. Eucalyptus acorns were ground up and used in food.

Eucalyptus trees have deep roots in the ground which absorb underground water. They live for a long time generally in groves and eucalyptus forests which grow in valleys, mesas and on some mountainside areas. Eucalyptus trees will continue to grow and thrive around the world. They are attractive and valuable trees.

TWENTY-TWO

The Bermuda Triangle

The Bermuda Triangle is located in Bermuda Island, the Bahamas and in Puerto Rico in the Atlantic Ocean and Caribbean Sea. It has been reported that airplanes and ships have disappeared in the Bermuda Triangle. It is believed that some magnetic force caused these airplanes and ships to sink to the bottom of the ocean.

However, a small number of airplanes and ships have disappeared in the Bermuda Triangle. Commercial flights pass through the Bermuda Triangle regularly without falling in the ocean.

UFO sightings occur in the Bermuda Triangle; especially at Puerto Rico. Atlantean ruins have been discovered in the Bermuda Triangle in shallow water. Three stone pyramids have been found here. One of the pyramids had a statue with a crystal with seven miniature pyramids.

The harbor at Bimini Wall was discovered. The continent of Atlantis had Sunk in this Bermuda Triangle. Rectangular buildings, marble pillars and small stone statues are at the bottom of the ocean. Some of these rectangular buildings were found off Andros Island. A blacktop paved road goes hundreds of miles under the ocean.

People shouldn't be afraid to go to the Bahamas, Bermuda Island and Puerto Rico even though these islands exist in the Bermuda Triangle.

In the bottom of the Bermuda Triangle botanists and geologists discovered tropical plants and remains of land animals. They found lava that had solidified only the way that it is possible to on the surface. This proves that Atlantis existed at one time.

TWENTY-THREE

Seances

Certain people are curious about loved ones who have passed on to the other side. They attend séances to find out about their departed, loved ones. They pay a psychic person to use a weegie board to make contact with deceased souls.

A psychic may turn the lights out and light candles to create a mysterious environment. The psychic claims to receive messages from the other side. The person seeking information about deceased persons tends to be vulnerable and naïve because he or she wants to believe what the psychic is communicating.

Quite often séances are not a way to seek truth about someone who has passed away. Psychism may not be accurate. It is a form of black magic. It may cause psychic entities to be attracted to the psychic. This is not emotionally healthy for the participants. Black Lodge agents may project thoughts into the psychic's mind to fool them. The psychic entities have access to the lower akashic records of the deceased persons.

Ignorant individuals should be leery and cautious about attending séances. They may find out some truthful information.

However, some of the information expressed to them may be false. False information may deceive them.

It is best to avoid séances because the wrong, psychic energy and forces may lead to a harmful result. Be glad to hold light around loved ones who are deceased. Detach yourself from their spirits. Allow them to continue on their journey within the other side without interfering with their psychic energy.

TWENTY FOUR

Playing An Organ

To play an organ takes special training in how to touch bass notes on foot pedals near the player's feet. An organist must learn how to play foot pedals and increase or decrease the volume of organ notes.

Some organs have three keyboards while other organs may have one or two keyboards. Larger organs have pipes attached to the organ so notes are even more melodic.

Organ keys must be sustained by holding the treble and bass keys down to maintain the sounds of the notes. There are many organ pieces arranged to play on the organ.

Frederic Handel, who composed The Messiah for church music, played the organ. Background organ music is played for this sacred music. Johannes Sebastian Bach composed many organ pieces.

The organ is played mainly in churches. Church music such as religious hymns are played on the organ by church organists. Organ music is melodic and soothing. Old fashioned organs had to be pumped to produce sound. Electric organs are primarily used today. They do not have to be hand pumped.

It is worthwhile and fun to play an organ. Organ music is rich and pleasant to listen to. So, learn to play an organ. This musical instrument is a popular instrument to learn to play.

———— TWENTY-FIVE ————

The Assembly

Many people gather at assemblies for special occasions. School assemblies generally take place once or twice a month. The school principal usually makes announcements. Then awards may be presented. Musical performances are presented such as choir music and orchestra music. Poetry may be recited. Certain classrooms may present skits and classroom projects to the audience.

People attend community assemblies at town halls especially during holidays and special occasions. Vocal soloists may perform. Duets and trios may be presented. Someone may present a speech about a stimulating topic.

People assemble together for special reasons. Talented performances entertain large audiences. A variety of entertaining activities are presented.

Judy Weatherly was a vocal soloist. She was a senior in high school. She also played the piano. Judy was asked to perform in an assembly. She sang <u>Strangers in Paradise</u> on a stage. A pianist accompanied Judy. Judy was nervous at first. She performed in front of 350 people. She almost forgot the words to this song. In fact, she stopped in the middle of the song. She decided to start over.

While Judy stood in front of the large audience, the auditorium was dark. A bright light was beaming on Judy. She was in the spotlight. Everyone was looking at her. Judy began the vocal solo again. She tried harder to remember the words of the song. She tried to overcome her fear of the audience. This time she sang the whole song. She made up some words to fill in the song.

The audience felt sympathetic towards Judy because they knew she had stopped once. They knew she was nervous. When Judy completed the solo the audience clapped. She was relieved that she was done singing. She walked off the stage after bowing several times. Her piano accompanist went off stage as well.

A group of high school students presented a puppet show. They moved the puppets on the stage and repeated dialogue for the puppets. The audience was amused. They laughed when some dialogue was humorous. The puppet show was very entertaining.

The high school choir performed next. The choral director directed the choir of 50 students after they lined up in rows on the stage. The choir sang three four part choir pieces. A piano accompanist accompanied the four part choir. They sang three modern, choral pieces. The audience clapped loudly after they performed each choral piece. The choir was dressed in black and white outfits.

When the assembly performance was over, the audience clapped very loudly with enthusiasm. The 350 people began leaving the auditorium. Judy Weatherly looked for her parents once the performers were excused to go home. School was out for the day.

Mr. and Mrs. Weatherly were standing at the back of the auditorium waiting for their daughter. Judy finally spotted them. She walked over to them. Her parents complimented Judy for her vocal performance. Judy blushed and said, "I didn't do very well. I forgot the words to the song!"

Mrs. Weatherly looked at her daughter with understanding. She said, "You had enough courage to start over! You finished the solo. We are proud of you." Judy felt better after she was praised by her mother. She planned to bring a small card with the words for the next song she was asked to sing. There would be another assembly in two weeks.

TWENTY-SIX

Settling In Pioneer Country

During the early days in America many pioneers traveled by canestoga wagons and by horses or by foot to the West. Prairie country existed in midwestern lands. Prairie lands were filled with tall grass and wild flowers.

Early pioneers traveled a long distance through rough terrain, passed lakes and streams, over rugged mountains, through forests and even deserts. Lewis and Clark explored the midwest and west in earlier days. The Oregon Trail was discovered.

Pioneers packed their belongings, cooking and camping equipment such as cooking utensils, pots and pans, ropes, sacks of beans, flour and sugar, buckets, containers of fruit and vegetables and tents with stakes, hammers, shovels and many more items.

Pioneers had to take care of their livestock such as horses, cows and some other animals. Some pioneers brought their pets such as dogs. The animals needed to be fed regularly. Horses, cows and cattle grazed in fields of grass. Barley was fed to the horses as well as some alfalfa when it was available.

The pioneers stopped at lakes and streams to drink water, catch fish and wash clothes. They enjoyed bathing and swimming in the clear, cool water. Often, fresh water fish were caught in the lakes and streams. The Sun gleamed in the lakes and streams with a sparkling effect.

When pioneers went through forests they had to be careful because there were wild animals. Bears, wolves, hares, squirrels, deer and various birds dwelled in forests. Campfires were lit especially at night to light up campsites to keep wild animals away.

Bears smelled campfire food and roamed into pioneer campsites. Pioneer men used guns to scare bears away from pioneer camping areas. They often had to shoot bears. Bear meat was eaten. Bear skins were saved and made into jackets and coats.

Buffaloes roamed in herds in prairie lands. Thousands of buffaloes existed in earlier days in America. Pioneer men shot buffaloes for meat and buffalo skins. They chased buffaloes until they came close enough to shoot them.

Rabbits were also hunted for rabbit meat. The pioneers needed meat as part of their food. They cooked beans, vegetables and ate wild berries. Salt brine was added to meat. Bacon was cooked for breakfast and served with beans.

Women and children gathered firewood, wild berries and other food such as mushrooms and watercress. They prepared the food at the pioneer campsites. They washed clothes at the streams and lakes. Men usually went fishing and hunting. They made fishing poles by cutting thin limbs into wooden poles. Then a fishing string was tied on the pole. Bait was put on hooks to throw into the streams or lakes to catch fish.

Once fish were caught they were placed in buckets of cold water to keep them fresh. Women cut up the fish and cleaned them. The fish was cooked over the campfires so the pioneers could eat them. They put salt on the fish.

Men skinned buffaloes and cut them up into chunks of meat. The buffalo meat was cooked over campfires. Buffalo skins were cleaned, cured and tanned. Then they were stretched and made into clothes. The pioneers depended on wild animals for food and to make clothing.

The pioneers faced many challenges and dangers as they traveled West across America. The weather changed from hot to cold, chilly temperatures. Pioneers traveled while it rained and snowed. It was difficult for them to travel over rugged mountains.

Many pioneers had to endure extremely cold winters as they traveled West to their destinations. American Indians were not always friendly. In fact, pioneers were attacked by Indians who did not want settlers passing through their lands.

Some pioneers were able to make friends with certain Indians in certain tribes. American Indians taught settlers to plant maize known as corn. They taught settlers their way of life in the wilderness. Unfriendly Indians tried to discourage settlers from settling in the Midwest and Western areas.

However, the American pioneers continued traveling West where they settled in the wilderness in prairies, near lakes and streams. They used forest trees to create logs so they could build log cabins. Pioneers sealed the logs with clay and hard mud. Log cabins were built with fireplaces so the pioneer settlers could keep their log cabins warm especially at night and during wintertime.

Fireplaces were also used for cooking meat, vegetables, soup, potatoes and bread. Large, iron pots were used to cook over the fire. The fireplaces also helped light up the log cabins. Parents read to their children near the fireplaces.

Pioneers endured many problems along the trails to the West. Their Conestoga wagons broke down along the way because of rough, rocky terrain. Wagon wheels had to be repaired so they could continue their long journey. Horses needed to be reshoed because their hooves wore down. Canvas tops on Conestoga wagons had to be resewn because of rips and tares.

Settlers in pioneer country had to be prepared for unexpected events and sudden changes. Weather conditions and rugged terrain made a difference regarding their progress on the long journey West. Once they settled in prairie lands they developed farms, ranches and small Western towns.

Today we are descendants of the American pioneers. Our American civilization grew and expanded in the midwestern territories and the west. We should appreciate the early pioneers and settlers who made it possible for Americans to live in prairie country.

TWENTY-SEVEN

Production Of Leather Goods

Leather goods are available in many stores, shops and market places in booths and tents. There are leather purses, wallets, bags, boots, shoes, jackets and coats.

There is an art and method in making different, leather goods. Purses and wallets are produced from cured, tanned leather that has been softened. The leather is shaped into a variety of purses and wallets. Other fabric designs are sewn into the leather. The purses and wallets are sewn carefully by hand or sewing machines.

Leather boots and shoes are made from cured leather that has been tanned and softened. The leather is shaped into boots and shoes. Hardened leather soles and heels are tacked on and glued on shoes and boots. Shoes are stained in different colors. Cushioning is put inside shoes and boots to help make shoes comfortable and easier to walk in.

Handbags shaped into bags are also made of softened leather. Water pouches are made of cured, softened leather. Water pouches are opened and then closed with leather pull-strings.

Leather jackets and coats are made with cured, softened leather. Jackets appear smooth and even shiny. Coats made of leather look good. Many people wear leather jackets and coats.

Belts worn around a person's waist are made of hard or soft leather. The leather is carefully cut into narrow strips and stained with different colors. Belts are worn with blue jeans, pants and slacks. Women wear leather belts with dresses, skirts and pants.

Leather goods are available around the world. Leather products are exported and imported in different nations, islands and countries.

TWENTY-EIGHT

Wineries

Grapes are grown in warmer climates around the world. Many grapes are grown in Italy, France, America and southern islands. Grapes are harvested and processed in wineries.

There are many wineries in Italy, France, California and some southern states of America. Each winery processes red and green grapes. Seeds are removed and the juice of the grapes is pressed to produce a pure, liquid juice. The juice is distilled and put into barrels and large containers to ferment. Once the grape juice is fermented for a period of time the aged grape juice is put into wine bottles and sealed with corks or tight lids.

Stored wine in bottles is labeled according to the type of grapes and taste of the wine. The wine bottles are stored in shelves in cool, large storage rooms in each winery.

Different wineries invite the public to taste their different red, purple and white wines. Each wine has a specific, unique taste and flavor. Some wines have become well known such as Burgundy, Napa white and red wine, Sonoma Valley Winery and San Joaquin Winery.

Wineries have existed for many years in different countries. Ancient civilizations produced wine in Rome, Greece, Sumeria, Egypt, Israel and other Middle Eastern countries. Wineries will continue to produce wine so that the public can buy wine at liquor stores, restaurants and bars, etc.

People buy wine to use at parties, special celebrations, at dinners and during other social occasions. Wine is a popular drink. Most wines contain some alcohol. Usually people sip one or two glasses of wine. They purchase wine at wineries, tasting rooms and grocery stores, etc.

— TWENTY-NINE —

American Colonies

American colonies existed at the East Coast of America. Thirteen colonies known as Vermont, Maine, Washington D.C., Virginia, Pennsylvania, North and South Carolina, New Jersey, Massachusetts, Maryland, Illinois, New York, Delaware and Michigan. These colonies were settled by early Americans who came to America in ships from England, France and Holland.

Early Americans came to the new land in America to escape from religious persecution, religious injustice and extremely rigid laws in Great Britain and other European countries.

Early colonies in America were small with a small population. Early colonists landed at Plymouth Rock on the East Coast. They cut down trees and created logs. They built Jamestown into a colonist village made out of logs and clay to seal the logs. Fireplaces were built in each log house. The houses were close together with a protective, log fence built around the village of Jamestown. Jamestown became a fort to protect early settlers.

Colonists banded together and shared food. Men in the colonies hunted turkeys, deer, rabbits, raccoons and they also went fishing in the ocean. Women in the colonies grew corn, vegetables and they cooked their daily food.

Life in the early, American colonies was difficult especially during cold winter months. Food was scarce. Some of the colonists died from starvation. Scurvy occurred because fruit was scarce.

Colonists had to find ways to survive harsh climates. They learned to store food for winter months. Corn became a food staple. American Indians taught American colonists to grow corn and vegetables. Colonists stored corn husks to eat during winter months. They kept meat in high storage places to dry and use for food during winter months.

Colonists had to be strong and brave to survive many challenges and dangers. They formed their first Parliament and began a independent government. George Washington led American patriots against English soldiers. Early colonists joined the first American army to fight for American freedom.

George Washington became the first American President. The American Preamble and Constitution was written, signed and used in America after Americans became independent from England. Early colonists were American forefathers. Our American forefathers were able to promote American independence and freedom. They risked their lives to establish America.

American colonists banded together to strengthen early America. They had courage and determination in order to survive. They wanted America to succeed, prosper and to expand and grow. Each colony continued to grow and finally the first thirteen colonies became the first thirteen American states. Eventually more American territories became American states. Today there are 50 states in America. Alaska and Hawaii became our last two American states.

The Louisiana Territory was purchased by Thomas Jefferson, America's third President. This large mass of land became the Midwestern and southern states in America. Many American colonists went west to settle in midwestern and western territories. They were no longer colonists.

—— THIRTY ——

Special Holidays

Special holidays are times when people in different cultures celebrate. There are religious holidays, patriotic holidays and other holidays. People celebrate holidays for saints, important leaders and holidays for St. Valentine's Day, Halloween, Christmas, New Years, Labor Day and Memorial Day, etc. St Patrick's Day and All Saints Day are celebrated.

Each holiday is for a specific purpose. Catholics have special holidays for saints. Different Catholic saints are St. Cecilia, St. Anne, St. Catherine and other saints. During holiday celebrations there are parades, feasts, mass for prayers and other festivities.

Patriotic holidays are Memorial Day, Presidents' Day and Martin Luther King Day. Memorial Day is set aside to remember soldiers who died during wars to defend Americans and other people from dangers from enemies. People go to soldiers' gravesites to commemorate their heroism and service to protect Americans and other people. Veterans Day is reserved to remember American veterans who served in major wars such as World War I and II, the Korean War and Vietnam War.

Labor Day is a special time to rest and take the day off from work. Most people have the day off. Some people go to parties and eat out. They are glad to have the day off and still get paid. Many people go on picnics and eat out to relax on their day off. Banks are closed and some businesses are closed. Students don't attend school on Labor Day.

The 4th of July is American Independence Day. America became freed from England in 1776. Americans celebrate on the 4th of July. Fireworks are lit up in the evening on this special day. Americans celebrate their independence from England on this patriotic holiday.

Christmas is usually celebrated for two weeks. On Christmas Eve young children believe Santa Claus will bring them gifts which they will open on Christmas Day. On Christmas Day most families open Christmas presents which have been kept under the Christmas tree. Christmas trees are decorated with colorful bulbs, a star and other dangling objects and lights. Christmas trees are usually beautiful to look at.

Christmas Day is a time to be with one's family. The family feasts on turkey, dressing, mashed potatoes, cranberry sauce, apple pie and eggnog. The families celebrate together especially during Christmas time. Most homes have decorated Christmas trees and other Christmas decorations are displayed indoors and outdoors. Many people are able to enjoy looking at many Christmas decorations. Christmas is a time to sing Christmas songs and to be merry.

New Year's Eve is a time to celebrate the New Year. At midnight there is loud cheering. Fireworks are lit up to celebrate the New Year. On New Year's Day most people celebrate the New Year. They have parties and parades. The Rose Garden Parade in Pasadena, California is a big event every year. Many roses are decorated on floats. Bands from different schools perform. Other floats with special themes are in the parade. Many people go to the parade or watch the Rose Parade on television.

THIRTY-ONE

Paradise Valley

Paradise Valley is any valley where the land is rich and fertile and where the weather is pleasant most of the time. Crops and fruit trees grow readily in the rich soil. Sunshine, as well as rain, brings successful, growing vegetables, fruits and other plants such as evergreen trees in groves and forests.

Paradise Valley is a safe, peaceful and harmonious place to live. Such a valley is not overpopulated. Homes are spread apart. Each home has a beautiful garden. All the gardens are well preserved and gardened so the plants thrive and flowers blossom readily. There are many magnificent views with verdant groves and forests. Many interesting birds and some harmless wild life exist in Paradise Valley.

People who live in Paradise Valley are friendly and neighborly. They get along with one another and serve one another. They want their valley to be a beautiful and wonderful place to live. People are happy in Paradise Valley because they enjoy its beauty plus sense of well being.

So, live in a harmonious place you can call your nirvana and utopia where people live in oneness with Nature and God.

THIRTY-TWO

Rolling Stones

Heavy stones have been rolled and moved around since ancient times. The Egyptians built many pyramids made with heavy stones and slabs step by step. Each stone slab was carefully placed into the pyramids to shape and hold them together. The stones were very heavy. Egyptians had hundreds of workers carry one large stone at a time to roll into place in the pyramid walls.

Ancient statues on Easter Island were pulled on slabs for miles to a special location near the ocean on Easter Island. These heavy stones were shaped into "gods" of the islanders which look out to sea. They appear to be waiting for beings in the sky or for someone to come across the ocean to Easter Island. The heavy stones were hoisted up and shaped into large, human figures with large faces and strange hats on their heads.

Ancient Tijuana culture in Peru and Bolivia moved very heavy stones into place step by step into walls and stone buildings. They may have used levitation to roll these immense, cut stones into an exact fitting stone by stone. These heavy stones have not been moved or destroyed by earthquakes.

Many of the pyramids in Egypt are still standing despite the harsh climate in Egypt. The stones are very heavy and solid. They have been very carefully put together to last.

Ancient Mayans built temples out of heavy stones. Their Mayan cities were built from heavy stones. Their temples still stand today. They must have rolled many stones into place to create their Mayan cities in Central America and Mexico.

Stones have been rolled and pulled for many years to be used for building stone temples, walls and for dwellings.

THIRTY-THREE

Exotic Melodies

Many exotic, interesting melodies have been composed or arranged from existing melodies. Melodies are played on guitars, the piano and by orchestras or bands. Solo instruments usually are used to play the melodies.

Some exotic melodies are TINY BUBBLES, MOON RIVER, BLUE HAWAII, MOONLIGHT SERENADE, MEMORIES, SOME LIKE IT HOT, CLOSE TO YOU, REMEMBER, AUTUMN LEAVES, IF I EVER LEAVE YOU, OKLAHOMA, KISS ME KATE, LOVE STORY, A SUMMER PLACE, THE BLUE LAGOON, YELLOW BIRD, I COULD HAVE DANCED ALL NIGHT, IF HE WALKED INTO MY LIFE, YOUNG AT HEART and many other songs.

Exotic melodies are still being composed and Sung around the world. People listen to the radio and television music programs. Each generation produces new music. The Beatles introduced different, exotic songs. Some of their songs were YELLOW SUBMARINE, YESTERDAY, ALL YOU NEED IS LOVE, LONG AND WINDING ROAD, A DAY IN THE

LIFE, HERE COMES THE SUN, LUCY IN THE SKY WITH DIAMONDS, NORWEGIAN WOOD, etc.

Vocal soloists such as Dean Martin, Tony Bennett, Andy Williams, Perry Como, Dinah Shore, Lena Horn, Nat King Cole, Cole Porter, Julie Andrews, Bing Crosby, Louie Armstrong, Sammy Davis Jr., Shirley Jones, Tony Martin, Elvis Presley, Karen Carpenter, Kate Smith, Jeanette MacDonald, Nelson Eddy and many more have sung interesting, melodic songs on radio, television and in movies.

THIRTY-FOUR

Skyscraper Majesty

Skyscrapers have been built in many large cities. New York City, Chicago, Detroit, Miami, San Francisco, St. Louis, Los Angeles, San Diego, Portland, Seattle, Dallas and Toledo all have skyscrapers.

The Empire State Building is the tallest skyscraper in New York City with 102 floors. At one time the tall tower buildings stood in downtown New York City. San Francisco is known for several tall skyscrapers. St. Marks is a tall skyscraper. Several business buildings are in the business district of this city.

Los Angeles has a variety of skyscrapers spread out in this city. The business district has more skyscrapers. Portland and Seattle have some skyscrapers. Seattle's Space Needle towers over many other buildings. San Diego has some skyscrapers which stand out. Dallas, Houston and Detroit have skyscrapers in their downtown districts. Hong Kong, London, Berlin, Paris, Stockholm, Lisbon, Warsaw, Madrid and Shanghai, etc. have skyscrapers. The tallest skyscraper at the turn of the 21st century is the one in Singapore. The tallest in the United States is the Sears Tower in Chicago.

Another huge skyscraper is in Taiwan. There is a report of plans to build the tallest skyscraper in Dubai.

Skyscrapers generally rise very high and are easily noticed. They have similar and different shapes. They stand out way above other buildings .Many skyscrapers have a majestic look with many windows and floors.

Skyscrapers must be earthquake proof. Any skyscraper that does not have a secure, earthquake, roof foundation is very dangerous. A skyscraper which topples can destroy other buildings and can damage and kill many people who are near the toppling skyscraper.

Well built skyscrapers do not fall to the ground. They should last for many, many years. Majestic looking skyscrapers add to the appearance of a city.

THIRTY-FIVE

Strawberry Bonanza

Strawberries grow in abundance in Fair Oaks, Arroyo Grande, Oceano and other regional fields. Strawberry fields are visible at The Pike and on Farrell Road in Halcyon and Grover Beach.

Strawberries are picked and put into boxes. A strawberry festival takes place usually once a year in Arroyo Grande, California. Many booths are set up with a variety of interesting items. Strawberries are served at the festival. Strawberries are served in strawberry short cake. Strawberry Sundaes are served. Scoops of strawberry icecream are served. Strawberry milkshakes are served as well.

Strawberries help bring prosperity to market places, strawberry stands and grocery stores. Strawberries are served in pies, cakes, custards, tarts and in fruit bowls. Strawberry festivals include entertainment such as solo bands played at gazebos and bandstands. A variety of activities take place such as special dance performances, Country Music solos and comedian acts.

Many people look forward to the Strawberry Festival in Arroyo Grande, California every year which usually takes place in July. Hot dogs, French fries, icecream, hamburgers and cold drinks are served.

People walk around to look at different booths so they can buy different items such as jewelry, clothing, hats, shoes, herbs, dark glasses, miniature objects such as glass menageries, gemstones, wrist watches and many more things.

Strawberry bonanzas are fun to participate in to celebrate strawberry harvests.

THIRTY-SIX

Flower Bouquets

Flower bouquets are arranged in a variety of ways with different flowers blended together. Each bouquet is designed in different sizes. Small bouquets are handed as special gifts to other people. Large bouquets are displayed on tables, at weddings, funerals and other celebrations.

Flower arrangements may hang from ceilings, high shelves and on the floor in special baskets. Flowers cheer up restaurants, social halls, churches, homes, offices, shops and other public places. Flower bouquets are displayed at outdoor events.

Flower bouquets are hand made arrangements which florists create. People in general can arrange bouquets for special occasions and for decorations. Roses, daisies, poppies, African violets, lilies, tulips, birds of paradise, sunflowers, daffodils, pansies, columbines and more are selected to create attractive, flower bouquets.

Flower bouquets are popular and have been arranged for many years. People enjoy looking at colorful flower arrangements.

THIRTY-SEVEN

Electing Politicians

Electing politicians, who follow through with their campaign promises, is important. Whoever becomes elected as President of the United States of America will make decisions that will affect many people. Election of congressmen and women, U.S. representatives and U.S. senators makes a difference in how our American government functions effectively.

If dishonest, corrupt politicians are elected, they can do a lot of harm to many people. Corrupt politicians lie to the public. They cover up their corruption. Some elected politicians misuse government money.

Some American presidents have tried to do a good job. George Washington promoted freedom and independence as America's first president. Abraham Lincoln promoted justice and equality. He abolished slavery and stopped corruption. He was concerned about American currency. He wanted to avoid inflation of American money.

John F. Kennedy established the Peace Corp. He attempted to investigate inflation of American dollars. Bill Clinton cleared up the national debt. He avoided wars. He tried to promote peace. He helped Haiti and Ireland to promote peace as well. Jimmy Carter avoided wars. He has helped promote housing and fair laws. He is concerned about the Palestine and Israel problem over use and ownership of land.

Barrack Obama has been initiating some positive changes. He has proposed a more universal health program for all Americans. He is promoting policies for educational improvement of our American environment and social justice. In six months he has tried to clear up economic issues and financial difficulties in American banks which were bankrupt. He has given money to the car industries in America to keep them afloat. He is concerned about the war in the Middle East. This ongoing problem has been a challenge in the Middle East.

Richard Nixon attempted to promote a good relationship with China. He went to China to open trade and better communications between America and China. Unfortunately, the Watergate scandal caused exposure of corruption in the Nixon Administration. Some of the politicians robbed the American treasury. Newspapermen from the Washington Post investigated corrupt politicians in the Nixon Administration.

Andrew Jackson fought for justice and honesty in his administration. He balanced the American budget and stopped political corruption. Franklin Roosevelt was selected three times as an American president. He established the New Deal. He promoted the Boy Scouts of America. He helped America come out of the Great Depression in the 1930s. America entered World War II during his leadership as our American president.

As a result World War II was won by the free world. Hitler's dictatorship was defeated. Germany and Japan surrendered in 1945.

Many of our U.S. representatives, senators and congressmen and congresswomen present propositions and policies about economic issues, environmental problems, health programs, education policies and many more issues. Propositions, policies and bills are presented. Then U.S. representatives, senators and congressmen and congresswomen vote yes or no on bills, propositions and policies.

It is important to vote for politicians who will do an effective job to make positive changes in our American government. We should elect honest, moral and effective American U.S. representatives, senators, congressmen and congresswomen as well as American presidents who will do a good job as American leaders.

THIRTY-EIGHT

At The Lagoon

Many birds flock to lagoons. Geese, ducks, seagulls, cormorants, herons, sparrows and mud hens fly over to a lagoon. They swim and move around in the lagoon looking for food. Geese, ducks and seagulls dip their heads into the water searching for insects and drifting, water plants.

Geese, ducks and seagulls gather in flocks. They like to be fed bread crumbs, popcorn, lettuce and other scraps. They nibble on grass and falling leaves. Geese, ducks and seagulls clean their feathers regularly.

Geese like to make honking sounds. Ducks like to quack. Seagulls make loud sounds. All of these birds communicate when they make their bird sounds. When the leader flies away the flock of geese, ducks and seagulls usually follow the leader. Sparrows also flock together. They peck at grass and seeds. They move about in trees near the lagoon.

The view of a lagoon is serene and picturesque. The calm, dark blue water is interesting to observe. Reeds and tullies grow around the lagoon adding to the beauty surrounding the calm water.

The water in a lagoon may change colors because of the changing colors in the sky. If the sky has gray clouds the lagoon reflects gray. If clouds are white and pink the lagoon reflects white and pink. Street lights and car lights reflect bright colors in lagoons.

Other wildlife such as raccoons, deer, elks and bears come to lagoons to drink water. Rabbits may dwell near some lagoons. They need lagoon water to drink. Lagoons usually come from ocean water which flows inland into a special area.

People like to have picnics near lagoons. Usually grass grows near the lagoon. People sit on the grass or at picnic tables and under shady trees to enjoy their picnics. The pleasant views at the lagoon are peaceful and beautiful.

THIRTY-NINE

Weekend Adventures

Many families, couples and individuals look forward to weekend adventures. They enjoy going to the beach to swim, snorkel, fish and walk on the beach. Some people like to go up into the mountains and hills to enjoy nature. Other people go to the zoo, to recreation parks such as Disneyland, Knottsberry Farm, Magic Mountain and Great America. Some people go camping and hiking while others go skiing and boating.

Jasmine Elderman and her husband, Peter Elderman worked in a family business from Monday to Friday, 8:00 a.m. to 5 p.m. They worked very hard in the family business.

On weekends Jasmine and Peter liked to relax and go places for adventures. Their favorite pastime was to go boating at lakes and the ocean. They were outdoors people. They liked to go walking and hiking in woodlands and meadows. They enjoyed sniffing fragrances of trees, wild flowers and grass.

The Eldermans took their 21 foot boat down to Lake Naciamento. They launched the boat into the lake. They had brought a packed lunch along and swimsuits so they could go swimming in the lake. They took their boat out into the middle of the lake. The water was a deep blue.

Jasmine decided to go swimming in the deep lake. She put on her swimsuit. She jumped into the cold lake and began floating in the cold water. She was shivering for some time because her body needed to adjust to a 50 degree temperature. Once Jasmine adjusted to the cold water she began to swim in the lake. Peter remained in the boat to keep an eye on the boat.

Peter finally threw an anchor into the lake. He put on his swimming trunks. He jumped into the lake and floated around at first. Then he swam over to Jasmine. They stayed close together and continued swimming. They swam for fifteen minutes.

Jasmine became tired. She swam back to the boat. Peter followed her to the boat. They both stepped back into their boat. Both of them decided to lie down on towels on the boat deck to Sun themselves. The Sun dried their skin and their swimsuits.

Peter and Jasmine decided to eat their packed lunch. Jasmine opened the package of food. There were tuna sandwiches with pickles, tomatoes, lettuce and mustard on rye bread. They munched on carrot sticks and ate potato salad. Then they sipped ice tea. Delicious cookies were eaten for dessert.

Jasmine and Peter continued to take the boat around sightseeing the lake after they ate lunch. They observed many sights from the lake to the landscape. It started to get dark; so, Jasmine and Peter stopped the boat and anchored it. They looked at a magnificent Sunset of brilliant crimson colors. Then the stars came out. They identified different constellations. They looked at the Big Dipper, The Pleiades, Orion, The Bear and other constellations.

The Moon came out and was shining brightly. It was a full Moon. Jasmine pointed to the Moon. She said, "I see a face on the Moon!" He smiled and said, "I see the face, too! "They both gazed at the Moon for some time.

At approximately 9:30 p.m. Jasmine and Peter decided it was time to go to bed. They rolled out bedrolls on the boat deck. They got into their bedrolls and laid there. They looked up at the stars until they fell asleep. During the night the full Moon moved across the sky. By morning the Moon had moved near the horizon.

Jasmine and Peter woke up when the Sun began to come up. They had slept well during the night. Jasmine prepared eggs, bacon, hash browns and toast and hot coffee for breakfast in a small kitchenette on the boat. The Eldermans ate their breakfast.

It was Sunday morning and Jasmine and Peter took the boat back to shore. They hooked the boat over the back of their truck. They drove through the countryside and saw beautiful meadows, groves and forests as well as wildflowers. Blue and purple lupins and orange poppies were growing in meadows along the way home.

When Jasmine and Peter were home Peter stored their boat in their garage. It was late in the afternoon on Sunday. Jasmine and Peter recalled their adventures that weekend. They had a wonderful time on the weekend.

FORTY

Life Of Wild Animals

Wild animals must learn how to survive. They must hunt for food and find a protective area to dwell. They need to find water. So, they dwell near lakes, streams and water holes. Wild animals must learn to defend themselves from their predators in order to stay alive.

Brown and black bears live in woodland areas, in mountainsides in caves and near streams and lakes. Mother bears look after their cubs for at least two years. Baby cubs nurse for a period of time. They begin to eat berries, honey and then meat as they grow. Mother bears protect their cubs from male bears, mountain lions and wolves. Cubs learn to hunt for food with their mother bears. After two years the mother bears leave their cubs. The two year old cubs must live on their own and find food for themselves. Bears hibernate during winter months.

Deer and elks live near woodlands so they can eat leaves off of trees. They eat scrubs and grass as well as ferns. Deer raise fawns. They sleep in bushes and near trees. The mother deer guards her fawns from bears and mountain lions. Bears tend to attack defenseless fawns.

Mother elks protect their baby elks. Deer, elks and moose provide milk for their young offspring. Baby deer, elks and moose stay close to their mothers. The mother deer, elks and moose ward off predators such as wolves, bears and other predators to protect their offspring. Some baby deer, elks and moose are killed and eaten by their predators.

Mother wolves and coyotes nurse their young, baby wolves and coyotes. Baby wolves and coyotes are helpless at birth. Generally, four baby wolves are in a pack. They must drink enough mother's milk to grow and be healthy. In time they eat meat, eggs, some wild plants and they drink water from streams. Wolves and coyotes tend to make wolf and coyote calls to communicate with other wolves and coyotes. Wolves live in groups and packs as a rule. They dwell in areas where wild animals live. They hunt for birds, raccoons, rabbits or hares, gophers, squirrels, etc. Wolves and coyotes are meat eaters. Coyotes and wolves howl to communicate to other coyotes and wolves.

Opossums live in trees. Their offspring cling to the mother opossum. They cling to the mother opossum's back. The mother opossum moves around in trees. Even on the ground a mother opossum guards her offspring. They continue to cling to the mother opossum for protection. Baby opossums drink milk from their mothers. Grown-up opossums hunt for bird eggs and small rodents for food.

Mountain lions live in the wilderness. They hunt for deer, elks, rabbits, foxes, rodents and baby bears. They chase after animals because they eat meat. Mountain lions roam in mountainsides and valleys looking for food. Mother mountain lions look after their offspring. Lion cubs nurse from their mothers.

Jungle animals must learn to survive in jungles in Africa, India and on other, tropical islands. Elephants live together. Baby elephants stay close to their mothers. Elephants eat jungle leaves and shrubs. They drink at water holes and streams. Mother elephants protect their offspring. Giraffes eat leaves from tall trees. Zebras roam in open landscapes as well. They eat fruit, leaves and shrubs.

Lions, tigers, leopards and black panthers hunt for antelopes, zebras, wild boars, anteaters, hyenas and birds, etc. Water buffaloes are hunted as well. The female lion and tiger generally hunt for food to feed their lion and tiger cubs. The male lion also eats what the female lioness has caught.

Monkeys, apes and sloths stay together and live in jungle trees. They eat jungle fruit such as bananas, jungle berries and some insects. Monkeys climb through the jungle trees. Mother monkeys protect their baby monkeys. They groom their offspring by pulling insects out of their hairy bodies. Mother monkeys and apes guard their offspring from predators.

Wild animals roam through savannahs. Savannahs can dry out during the dry season. Water holes dry out. Animals die because of the lack of water.

Wild animals continue to live in the wilderness. They must learn how to survive despite all dangers and challenges. Survival occurs for the stronger species. Weaker animals die out and do not survive usually. Some wild animals are becoming extinct. They must have enough food and water to survive.

Jungles, woodlands and savannahs need to be protected so wild animals can live and survive in the wilderness.

FORTY-ONE

A Positive Outlook On Life

A positive outlook on life makes a difference in each person's life. Positive thoughts are more constructive than negative thoughts. Positive thoughts and actions change the lives of people who are affected by them.

When a person develops a positive attitude about daily life he or she is able to accomplish much more each day and night. Positive feelings and accomplishments strengthen a person emotionally, physically and spiritually. Positive thinking helps a person fulfill his or her goals and aspirations.

Michelle Gibbons was having difficulty at home with her husband. She was challenged because her husband was burdened with cancer. He had lost his job at the factory. He was laid up at home. Michael Gibbons was discouraged and depressed because he had cancer and he had lost his job, which had provided money to pay for living expenses. Michael had developed a negative attitude because of his circumstances.

Michelle felt downcast because of her husband's problems. She decided to seek advice and help from her pastor at her local church. She went over to his office at her church. Pastor Williams was sitting at his desk when she arrived at his office doorway.

Michelle tapped on the pastor's office door. Pastor Williams looked up and glanced at Michelle. She asked, "May I come in?" Pastor Williams replied, "Please come in." Michelle entered her pastor's church office. She looked at Pastor Williams with deep concern. Pastor Williams asked, "What can I do for you Michelle?" Michelle said, "I need your advice Pastor Williams."

Pastor Williams said, "Please sit down." Michelle sat in a chair across from the pastor. She continued, "My husband, Michael has lost his job. To top it off he has cancer. I don't know what to do!" Pastor Williams asked, "Have you prayed to Jesus?" Michelle replied, "I have been too upset to pray."

Pastor Williams spoke. "You are going through a challenging time. You are being tested. Start praying for strength and guidance. Jesus will help you through this rough time. You must have faith in Jesus and yourself." Michelle thought about what Pastor Williams advised. She responded, "It isn't that easy. My mind is mixed up and I get depressed about the future."

Pastor Williams spoke. "You must develop a positive outlook and attitude in order to help you to forgive and accept your husband's problems. He needs your strength and faith in God and Jesus to overcome his predicament. Pray that he will be cured of cancer. In time he may find another job. You must not give up."

Michelle began crying. Tears flowed down her cheeks. Pastor Wiliams said, "Let it all out. You will feel better. Perhaps you can find a job to help pay your living expenses. You should take Michael to the best cancer clinic so he can receive the best treatment for his cancer. Michelle stopped crying. She wiped the tears off her face.

Michelle looked at Pastor William's and said, "I will do what you advise me to do." Pastor Williams said, "Let's pray to Jesus and God together." Pastor Williams bowed his head. Michelle also bowed her head. He said, "Heavenly Father, we ask you to guide and heal Michael and Michelle Gibbons in their time of need. Heal Michael from cancer. Help him find another job. We have faith that you will protect Michelle and Michael. Amen."

Pastor Williams raised his head. Michelle raised her head as well. Pastor Williams said, "Have faith and belief that God will show you the way. Continue to pray for guidance and protection." Michelle looked at her minister and said, "Thank you for your advice and prayers."

Michelle stood up. She left Pastor Williams' office and went to her apartment. She continued to pray for guidance and help. Michelle checked around for the best cancer clinic in her regional area. She called the cancer clinic to enroll her husband, Michael. The administrator asked if her husband was insured with Medical Insurance.

Michelle said, "My husband was covered with Medical Insurance from his employer. She didn't mention that he was no longer working for an employer. Michelle was worried that if she told the administrator her husband was unemployed he would not be accepted at the cancer clinic. The administrator told Michelle to bring her husband to the cancer clinic.

Michelle began to feel hopeful about her husband receiving medical care for his cancer condition. She spoke to her husband and told him to come with her in their car to the cancer clinic. He reluctantly responded. She managed to get him in her car. She drove to the cancer clinic in another town.

Michelle and Michael walked into the cancer clinic. Michelle filled out some forms at the front desk. She picked a number and Michael and Michelle waited in the sitting room for their number to be called. After 43 minutes Michael's name was called. Michelle and Michael went into another room and waited for a cancer specialist to diagnose Michael's condition. Finally a doctor came into the room. He examined Michael closely and asked some questions.

Dr. Sharkey asked, "How long have you had cancer?" Michael replied, "I think I have had cancer for around three months." Dr. Sharkey asked, "How did you find out that you have cancer?" Michael replied, "I was X rayed at a hospital three months ago. The results of the X-rays indicated I have cancer."

Dr. Sharkey said, "You need more X-rays so I can trace how far the cancer has spread. You may need radium treatments right away." Michael looked glum. Michelle spoke. "Michael, you should have radium treatments." Dr Sharkey continued, "You should begin radium treatments immediately so we can eliminate cancer cells and keep them from spreading."

Michael frowned and replied, "Will my hair fall out? Dr. Sharkey replied, "Don't worry about your hair. The important thing is for us to have the cancer treated and put in remission. We may be able to stop the cancer from growing."

Michelle looked at her husband, Michael with a hopeful look. She said, "The radium treatments may stop the cancer. You may be able to recover. You must accept the radium treatments." Michael looked at his wife and realized that she was probably right. He told Dr. Sharkey he would accept radium treatments. Michelle was relieved that her husband was willing to accept medical help.

Dr. Sharkey set up a daily schedule for radium treatments. Michael was asked to come to the cancer clinic from Monday through Friday from 10 a.m. to 12 noon for treatments. Michael began radium treatments the next morning. He came back five days a week for six months. Michelle kept praying he would recover from cancer.

Meanwhile, Michelle became a waitress in order to pay the bills. She received tips as well as $8.00 an hour as a waitress. She worked 40 hours a week. She was able to pay the rent which was $800 a month. She usually received several hundred dollars for tips beyond her monthly wages. She had enough to buy groceries.

Michelle prepared nutritious meals for Michael and herself. Michael rested in order to help recover from cancer. He began to feel better. Michelle continued to work as a waitress for five years. She continued to go to church on Sundays. She prayed to Jesus Christ and God.

In time, Michael's cancer was in remission. Radium treatments stopped cancer cells from spreading. Old cancer cells were killed. Michael was finally restored after several years. He began to be more hopeful. Michael eventually found another job. He was able to work regular hours in an office as a bookkeeper.

Michelle and Michael were able to pay their bills and even save some money for emergencies. They were getting along better in their personal lives. They had learned to think positive thoughts. They had faith in God and Jesus Christ because Michael attended church regularly with Michelle. He became a Christian. He had developed a positive outlook on life because Michelle encouraged him to think positive thoughts and to develop positive attitudes and goals.

FORTY-TWO

Forest Wonders

Forest wonders exist around the world in many countries. Forests are quite majestic and beautiful. Each tree adds to the unique beauty of a forest. Some trees are taller than other trees.

The leaves on trees may change colors. Evergreen trees are green year round. Forests can be seen for miles. They hold soil down and protect the land where they grow.

Butterflies fly around in the forest trees adding color and wondrous beauty to a forest. Each forest has a certain amount of trees. Some forests are near the coastline near the ocean. Other forests grow inland near meadows and lakes.

Each forest usually attracts wildlife. Animals find shelter and protection in forests. Wild animals find food in forests. Squirrels make their nests in tree branches. Woodpeckers peck and hammer deep holes in tree trunks to make their nests. Forest trees provide a home for many birds. Robins, finches, blue jays, blackbirds, sparrows and quail dwell in forests.

Sunshine beams through forest trees. The light of Sunrays creates colors and light in forests. Forest wonders exist in every forest. Many fragrances permeate forests. Tree bark changes color and peals off of tree trunks. Tree branches spread out and blend in the forest creating many designs worth looking at. Forest wonders are magnificent.

FORTY-THREE

Sunset Boulevard

Sunset Boulevard in Hollywood is a major street. Sunset Boulevard is at least 15 miles long. Drivers travel east or west. So they drive directly toward the Sun. They see the sunset at the end of each day. Sunsets in Hollywood are brilliant with crimson colors.

Many attractions exist on Sunset Boulevard. There is the Laugh Factory that is a world famous, comedy club on Sunset Boulevard. The Whiskey A Go Go is the most famous rock-in-roll and blues nightclub. Many exotic restaurants exist on Sunset Boulevard.

Mel's Diner is a famous 1950s restaurant. Many people eat at Mel's Diner. Famous recording studios exist on Sunset Boulevard. During the 1960s Sunset Boulevard was the most famous street for famous musicians. Sunset Boulevard goes all the way to the Pacific Ocean.

During the 1960s Sunset Boulevard was known as the headquarters for "The Summer of Love." Every night there is a variety of entertainment on Sunset Boulevard. There are glittering lights on Sunset Boulevard.

Many people drive their cars up and down Sunset Boulevard to see the lights and many attractions. Sunset Boulevard is one of the most famous boulevards in the world.

———— FORTY-FOUR ————

Summer Delights

We look forward to summer delights when we experience warmer weather and have time off from school and work. There are many things to do especially during summer months.

Barbara Sterling looked forward to summertime. She was a junior in college. She worked hard during the school months as a student. Summertime was a time for her to relax and enjoy other activities. She had time to experience adventures and have exciting, wonderful times.

Many adventures are available for a person who wants to experience the joy of life. Barbara was an adventurous person. She liked to hike in the hills and mountainsides, go bicycle riding, swimming, camping and to recreation centers and parks, to the theaters and to national parks. Barbara liked to go boating in the ocean and in lakes. She even liked to ski on snowcapped slopes.

Barbara decided to travel abroad during her summer vacation. She took an air flight to Switzerland and stayed in a mountain village not far from Lucerne. Barbara stayed in a cabin close to woodlands. Wild animals roamed around near her cabin. Barbara observed mountain goats on mountain ledges. Cows walked through the mountain village with bells clanging as they walked down the main street of the village.

Chalet houses made out of wood were visible everywhere. Chalet houses usually were two stories with balconies. Potted flowers were arranged on the balconies. The air was cold and crisp as well as fresh. Barbara walked into the village to enjoy shops and cafes.

Barbara walked into a dress shop and looked around at Swiss sweaters, coats and traditional Swiss outfits. She tried on some sweaters and Swiss outfits. She decided to buy a warm, yellow sweater and a Swiss outfit which had a blue center and white, long-sleeved blouse. Red and gold flowers were embroidered in the blue center of this outfit.

After Barbara purchased the sweater and Swiss outfit she left this shop. She continued walking down the cobblestone street. She came to a Swiss bakery. She stepped into this bakery. She saw hot-cross buns, pastries, made of flour dough with fruit inside. She saw Swiss chocolate cake and tarts.

Barbara was hungry. She bought some fruit tarts and hot-cross buns. She sat at a table at the side of the bakery room to eat her pastries. She also drank a cup of hot chocolate with whipped cream. The pastries and hot chocolate filled her up. She left the Swiss bakery satisfied and she continued walking down the cobblestone street. Their cow bells continued to ring. Barbara came to a clock shop. She was fascinated with this clock shop. She walked into the clock shop.

Barbara browsed around the clock shop and looked at a variety of Swiss clocks. Many of these clocks had dancing, miniature dolls and miniature animals which came out of the clocks at the hour or half hour. Barbara selected a clock with dancing, miniature Swiss dolls. The shopkeeper wrapped the clock in a box to protect it. Barbara took the wrapped clock along with her other packages out of the clock shop.

It was time for Barbara to go back to her rented cabin. She needed to rest. She built a fire with logs and paper. The flickering, burning logs in the fireplace were warming up the cabin. Barbara sat near the fireplace and watched the embers of the burning logs. She was warmed up by this comforting fire. She thought about her adventures in the village. She planned to eat dinner at a Swiss café later.

Barbara listened to Swiss music from a radio in her cabin. After she rested for awhile she dressed up in her new Swiss outfit and warm, yellow sweater. She put on a warm fur coat. She wore long, warm stockings with leather shoes. Barbara walked back to the mountain village.

The Swiss people were celebrating in the streets for a Swiss holiday. They were wearing traditional, Swiss clothes. Many of these Swiss villagers were dancing in the street to Swiss music. Some Swiss men were playing very long Swiss horns. Swiss folksongs were Sung by the Swiss villagers.

Swiss fondue with cheese and wine were served with bread chumps which were dipped into the fondue and eaten. Swiss beef and noodles with steamed vegetables were served at tables in the street. Homemade biscuits and Swiss cakes were served with this meal. Swiss families and elderly, Swiss people sat at the tables to enjoy the food.

A Swiss parade, with Swiss people dressed in traditional costumes, strolled down the street. Farmers and woodcutters were in the parade in their special costumes. Horn blowers paraded down the cobblestone street. Some Swiss dancers presented Swiss folk dances in the street.

The Swiss celebration went on for hours. A Swiss smorgasbord was given later in the day. Meatballs with spaghetti and a variety of sliced, Swiss cheeses were served. Meatloaf and salads were served. A variety of Swiss pastries were served for dessert. Many Swiss villagers selected food from the smorgasbord. They sat at long, outdoor tables to eat the delicious food.

The night sky was clear and many stars could be seen glittering in the sky. Light from the Moon beamed down on the mountain tops and slopes. Snow covered slopes were gleaming white. This white, gleaming snow could be seen for many miles away.

When the smorgasbord was over it was time to cleanup.

Folk dancing took place in the street. Barbara joined in dancing Swiss folk dances. She wanted to celebrate in the street by dancing with other Swiss performers. When everyone had danced for hours it was time to go back to their homes and dwelling places.

Barbara went back to her cabin at 9:30 p.m. that night. She rekindled the fireplace to warm up her cabin. She went to bed early that night to prepare for the next day. The next day after breakfast, Barbara dressed in her ski clothes and ski shoes. She took her pair of skis and went to a ski slope at the nearby mountain. She went skiing down the snow covered slopes. She was a good skier. She moved gracefully with ease up and down many slopes. She could see a view of the snow covered area. The sky was a clear blue. Yet, it was cold on the slopes. Barbara skied for an hour and a half. She enjoyed skiing because she felt a sense of freedom from skiing.

Barbara went skiing every day for a week. She met other skiers at the mountain slopes. She went to a Swiss ski lodge to socialize with other people who came to the slopes. She met some interesting people while she was there.

When Barbara returned home in America at the end of the summer she recalled her delightful, summer vacation in the Swiss Alps and quaint mountain village. She planned to return to this pleasant place again in the future because she had such a wonderful time.

FORTY-FIVE

Reverse The Aging Process

You can reverse the aging process which is known as "secondary aging." Aging causes creaking joints, poor vision, dull hearing and an awful tired feeling.

Life has been extended in the 20th and 21st centuries. In the Roman Empire people lived only about 24 to 30 years. In 1850, the average American died at age 45. By 1900 people lived to be 48 to 50. Today the average lifespan is 76.5 years. People live over 85 as well. There are over 40,000 people over 100 years old in the United States of America. By 2020 there may be more than 250,000 people who will have lived over 100 years.

Today, at age 70 and above people go back to school. They take trips and they even lace their walking shoes for a daily walk. If we reduced the number of deaths because of cancer and heart disease life expectancy will jump immediately from 75 to 85 years.

We want to be healthy and happy for as long as possible. The overwhelming message from recent research is that crippled hands, labored steps and bowed shoulders have more to do with inactivity and disease than getting older. Aging can be slowed down.

Good health habits are about eating right, exercising, looking good, abandoning bad habits and keeping your mind and attitude alert and keen. Natural, organic vegetables and fruits are nutritious to eat. Exercise regularly every day.

Why do we age? When cells and molecules become unstable they are out of balance because the free radicals cause less oxygen to circulate in human cells. In the human body, free radicals are a natural by-product of eating, breathing and expanding energy. Most of the time they are harmless, as long as your body stays in charge of the process. When it loses control, free radicals damage cell walls, attack chromosomes and DNA (the body's basic chemical structure), cause cancer or flat out assassinate our body cells. They also attack proteins in the lens of the eye, clouding it and causing cataracts, another curse of aging. They may oxidize the "so-called bad" cholesterol in the arteries, creating a plague buildup that stops the free flow of blood and prompts a heart attack or stroke.

It is important to remember that without antioxidants the human body wouldn't last five minutes in this oxygen-rich atmosphere of ours. They are absolutely crucial for life as we know it.

Too much vitamins is dangerous. It is known as beta-carotene, known as pro-vitamin A which is safe if taken in the proper amounts. 25,000 International Units (IU) is considered a safe daily dose for most adults, except pregnant women, who shouldn't get more than 6,000 I.U. One sweet potato provides about 25,000 I.U.

Vitamin C is a miracle worker. Citrus fruits provide Vitamin C. High levels of C and E in the blood counteract the effects of the major air pollutant, nitrogen dioxide. Sources of Vitamin C exist in orange juice, papayas, grapefruit juice, guavas, kiwi fruit, oranges, raw Brussels sprouts, raw green bell peppers, chili peppers, raw broccoli, collard greens, kale, strawberries and tangerines. We need 500 milligrams a day of Vitamin C.

Vitamin E is a fatty acid, the natural antioxidant in vegetable oils. Some people use Vitamin E capsules to heal rashes. Vitamin E is in the cell walls of the human body. Vitamin E works with Vitamin C to counteract oxidation of the lens and retina. Vitamin E boosts our immune system, trapping nitrates, which is a by-product of tobacco smoke. Vitamin E keeps them from becoming cancerous nitrosamines and it strengthens cell walls.

A very large study in Finland showed that people with high levels of Vitamin E in their bloodstreams had a lower incidence of cancer and far fewer cancer deaths than the rest of the population. Vitamin E offers powerful protection against heart disease by helping to keep blood cholesterol at a healthy level. It does that by preventing free radicals from oxidizing LDL (low-density lipoprotein) cholesterol the "bad" cholesterol which actually isn't so bad until the free radicals find it.

Vitamin E is a skin preserver slowing down the wrinkling and drying effect of the aging process. Sources of Vitamin E are in whole grains, vegetable oils, wheat germ oil, Sunflower seeds, almonds and raw wheat germ. You should take around 200 IU a day. Don't take more than 600 IU a day.

Glutathione is an enzyme made up of three amino acids, which are the building blocks of proteins. Glutathione not only scavenges free radicals, but donates its electrons to the free radicalized vitamins as well. This turns the vitamins back into antioxidants and lets them go about their business of doing us a world of good.

Glutathione is a potent cancer fighter, one of the most powerful allies the body has. It also knocks out free radicals in the lens and retina of the eye, helping prevent both cataracts and macular degeneration. Sources of glutatathione are fresh red, green and yellow vegetables plus smaller amounts in meat and poultry. You should have at least 250 milligrams per day, an amount you receive from five daily servings of fresh fruits and vegetables.

Selenium is a mineral nutrient that the body must have to create glutathione. Selenium is an anti-oxidant, working with Vitamin E to scavenge free radicals. It is an anti-cancer agent. Sources of selenium are mushrooms, garlic, radishes, carrots, cabbage, whole grains, broccoli, celery, cucumbers, shellfish, fish, red meat and poultry. 50 to 70 micrograms daily, although an adult is safe supplementing up to 350 micrograms a day.

Your body uses zinc to make a wide variety of antioxidant enzymes. There is proof that zinc works as an anti-oxidant on its own. Sources of zinc are seafood such as oysters, liver, beef, poultry, eggs, cheese, legumes and whole grains.

There are at least ten B vitamins. Your eyes need plenty of B vitamins. Without enough B-1 your optic nerves begin to degenerate. Without enough B-2 the degeneration speeds up.

Without enough B-12 you can harm the optic nerve. B-1, B-2, B-3, B-6 and B-12 help your digestive system tap into the energy in carbohydrates. These B vitamins are essential for healthy nerve fibers and skin.

Brain functions such as concentration, problem solving, memory and mood depend on an adequate supply of B-1, B-2 and folate (folic acid). Sources of Vitamin B are fortified cereals, breads, dairy products, meats, dry beans, peas, bananas, avocados, beef liver and clams.

Vitamin C holds your body together. It forms collagen, the connective tissue protein that makes up the walls of every cell in your body. Vitamin C is especially concentrated in the bones and in the cartilage, ligaments and tendons that cushion your bones and knit them together. Vitamin C is essential in the absorption of iron, the mineral your body needs to make the red blood cells that carry oxygen.

Your brain needs Vitamin C to make serotonin and norepinephrine, neurotransmitters that carry messages between brain cells. Like the B vitamins, vitamin C helps make protein go to work in your body. It also helps metabolize the B vitamin folate.

Vitamin D is a "Sunshine vitamin" and it is connected to the immune system in the bones. Bone marrow is important. Marrow is where the white blood cells are nurtured after they are produced in the thymus, spleen and lymph glands.

A vitamin D deficiency means you have a depressed immunity. Sunlight provides Vitamin D. Your intestines need vitamin D to absorb calcium, the prime ingredient in strong bones. One reason older people acquire bone thinning conditions osteomalacia and osteoporosis is because their diets lack enough Vitamin D and calcium. Aging may cause inefficiency in extracting nutrients. Some older people do not get out in the Sun enough.

Too much Sun is not good either. You need at least 10 to 15 minutes of Sun several times a week. You need twice as much Sun at 80 as at age 20. Sunlight on the skin stimulates a skin chemical which is converted into Vitamin D by the liver and kidneys.

Vitamin D also helps to prevent breast and colon cancer and deafness that involves tiny bones of the middle ear. It can also help control diabetes in older people. Sources of Vitamin D are in fortified dairy products, salmon, sardines, herring, eggs and chicken liver. Don't take more than 400 to 600 IU of Vitamin D.

An overdose of Vitamin D will cause too much calcium to get into your blood. This can cause kidney stones, bone loss, abdominal pain, nausea, vomiting and excessive urination.

Vitamin E reduces the blood's clotting ability by keeping platelets from sticking together. Vitamin E may help prevent heart attacks and strokes caused by blood clots plugging up arteries. This vitamin also protects the epithelial cells that line the arteries. Where there are deposits of cholesterol, fat and platelets which accumulate and form plaque, arteries may narrow dangerously.

Minerals are inorganic elements necessary for good health. They are a vital part of maintaining a variety of bodily functions which includes regulation of heart rhythm, bone formation and digestion. Boron produces bone-building Vitamin D, calcium and phosphorous. It helps keep bones from losing calcium and other minerals. Sources of boron are almonds, dates, hazelnuts, honey, peanuts, prunes, raisins, fruits and leafy vegetables.

Calcium is the most abundant mineral in your body. Calcium is in your bones, teeth and it is essential for blood clotting, nerve and muscle functions, including the nerves and muscles of the heart. It transforms food to energy and regulates blood pressure.

Your bones serve as a frame for your body. They serve as your body's mineral bank. If calcium is lacking bones become brittle and porous. A person shrinks in size and height. A person's bones can break easily. After menopause some women do not produce enough estrogen, which conserves bone calcium.

By cleaning the blood vessels and helping the body get rid of sodium, calcium plays a role in regulating blood pressure. Getting enough calcium to avoid bone and tooth loss also has a beauty effect. Calcium can keep your lips from turning inward and looking thin which causes aging and calcium deficiency. Sources of calcium are in non-fat yogurt, reduced fat cheese, nonfat milk, sardines, lackstrap molasses, almonds, cabbage, collard greens, beet greens, spinach and broccoli. You should have at least 1,000 to 1,500 milligrams per day. Teenagers and pregnant women should have at least 1,200 milligrams daily.

Chromium is an essential mineral to help your body's insulin regulate blood sugar levels. Chromium lowers "bad" (LDL) cholesterol. Sources of chromium are in Brewer's yeast, whole grains, liver, poultry, beef, potatoes with skin, fruit and vegetables.

Copper is an essential ingredient of an enzyme that makes hemoglobin. A deficiency of copper can lead to anemia. Sources of copper are in lobster, black pepper, coca, nuts, seeds, whole-wheat bran, beans, peas, vegetables and fruits.

Iron produces energy in your entire body. Stress, menstruation and heavy exercise can drain iron from your body which prevents the manufacture of hemoglobin, the substance in red blood cells that carries oxygen to all parts of the body. Lack of hemoglobin can cause anemia, exhaustion, lack of concentration and loss of appetite. This can make you feel older than you have to. Your body makes 2.5 million red blood cells every single second. Sources of iron are in red meats, poultry, green vegetables, nuts, cast iron cookware and fortified cereals. Vitamin C helps the body absorb iron from non-meat sources. Calcium and caffeine inhibit iron absorption from any source. Too much iron can cause heart disease.

We need magnesium which metabolizes energy in our bodies. Magnesium produces heart health. Magnesium keeps our blood pressure in check. It prevents clots from forming in the blood vessels, thus lowering the risk of stroke and heart attacks. Sources of magnesium are in soybeans, almonds, cashews, dry peas, lima beans, lentils, oyster, nuts, seeds, tofu and whole grains.

Potassium works with magnesium and calcium to keep muscles, including the heart, in top shape. It keeps the heartbeat steady and balances sodium to maintain the body's water balance. It keeps blood pressure under control.

Selenium is important for the health of your muscles, red blood cells, hair and nails. It helps counteract the toxicity of heavy metals like cadmium, mercury and silver. Selenium protects against heart disease, arthritis, sexual dysfunction and aging.

Our skin holds 20 percent of our body's zinc. Zinc helps the body get rid of carbon dioxide and is needed for wound-healing and bone-building. Vitamin A needs zinc to be able to make visual purple, the pigment your retinas need to have night vision. Zinc deficiency can play a role in senility.

Zinc plays a big role in men's fertility. The prostrate gland stores large amounts of zinc and male ejaculate contains several milligrams. A diet deficient in zinc can cut ejaculate levels by up to one-third.

In order to slow down aging we need to eat enough fiber foods, fish, vegetables and fruits. Garlic contains B-1, calcium, iron, potassium, phosphorous, zinc and selenium. Garlic is an antibiotic. Garlic is a potent virus fighter, protecting against flu. Garlic cuts cholesterol levels and reduces our risk of heart attacks and strokes. Garlic is a cancer fighter. Sources of garlic are fresh or freeze-dried garlic is best. The Kyotic and Kwai brands of garlic pills may contain enough allicin to be effective, although processing to remove the odor also generally removes most of the allicin. A Garlic extract and garlic oil are other ways to get allicin.

Ginger, ginseng and Brussels Sprouts all have valuable vitamins to control blood pressure. Substances in ginger have been shown to help stimulate the heart, to raise low blood pressure and lower high blood pressure. Ginger helps digestion by increasing hydrochloric acid and other stomach acids which tend to decline with age and by decreasing nausea and gas. Ginseng increases in mental awareness, memory, learning ability and concentration under the influence of ginseng. Ginseng can increase hand-eye coordination. This root also helps many people cope with stress, ironing out the highs and lows. Ginseng helps present anemia, atherosclerosis, high blood pressure and fatigue. Sources of fresh ginseng root, Siberian and Korean capsules are usually the best. Avoid liquid preparations that contain alcohol. Brussels sprouts contain significant amounts of the antioxidants Vitamin A and C. Brussels sprouts help to prevent cancer.

Exercise daily by walking, jogging and doing other physical exercises. Get plenty of Sunshine. Eat fresh, raw vegetables and fruits. Eat a wide variety of healthy foods. Think positive thoughts. If you maintain a healthy body you will feel younger and look younger.

FORTY-SIX

Balance Your Check Book

Each month it is important to balance your checkbook. Each check written should be recorded in your checkbook ledger. You should subtract each check amount from the total left in your checkbook. When you subtract each check carefully and accurately you will be able to know what money is still in the bank.

When our bank statement comes each month you should check off each check on the bank statement which was recorded and processed. Make a check in your ledger for each check processed. If your ledger doesn't tally and balance with your bank statement you should check for errors. You may have forgotten to subtract correctly. You may have not recorded automated checks from your bank account. You may have forgotten to add credits to your bank account in your ledger.

It is important to keep an accurate bank account so that you will not bounce any checks. Keep enough money in your checking and savings accounts so you will not run out of necessary money.

Bankruptcy occurs when a person runs out of money in their bank account. People file for bankruptcy when they are completely broke. Bills can be paid on a monthly plan.

Accurate bookkeeping is vital in order to balance your checkbook. You will be more successful if you balance your checkbook correctly.

FORTY SEVEN

Up-To-Date Computers

Up-to-date computers are needed because they operate much better than older computers. Well known computers are APPLE, IBM, and Dell Computers These computers have been around for some time.

Japanese computers are being produced and used. Up-to-date computers have more features. If a manuscript has been recorded in a modern computer each page can be seen in miniature form. Many pages show up on the screen.

Reports and manuscripts as well as letters can be properly formatted on up-to-date computers. Use GOOGLE to look up specific information. Visual materials and music can be on the up-to-date computers.

Up-to-date computers are useful in business offices to compute mathematics, statistics, graphs and charts. Geometric designs and geographical illustrations can be seen on computers. A lot of reference and resource materials can be located on an up-to-date computer.

It is worth keeping an up-to-date computer in your home. You will have access to a wide variety of information and resources. You can send anything you process on your computer electronically to far away places.

FORTY-EIGHT

Unusual Experiences

Unusual experiences may take place when we least expect it. Many unusual memories may go through our minds when we expand our consciousness and go beyond ordinary experiences. Rare opportunities can open up in our lives when we become alert and awakened to unusual relativities.

Cherish Longgate was traveling in a passenger airplane to a destination in the Hebrides Islands in 2012. Little did she know that she would encounter some rare and unusual experiences. While she was gazing out the airplane window to look at clouds in the daylight sky, she suddenly saw a UFO moving near the airplane.

Cherish became excited and eager when she saw this, large, saucer like object moving parallel in the same direction as the airplane she was traveling in. She continued to observe the UFO hovering near the airplane. The saucer-shaped UFO was silver with blinking red, green and yellow lights beaming from its center. Many windows were near the center of the large craft.

Cherish began to feel concerned why this saucer-shaped craft was following her air flight. She thought about the beings who were in the UFO. She wondered what they looked like. Within minutes a beaming light surrounded the airplane she was in. The airplane was lifted up into the UFO craft.

Everyone in the airplane was afraid and became hysterical because they felt helpless because the airplane now was inside the enormous UFO. They were afraid they were in danger and might be harmed. A ray of light was sent into the airplane and all the passengers, pilots and airline stewardesses became immobilized. They were unable to move.

When all the passengers were made helpless and defenseless some beings from the UFO craft entered the airplane. It was as if time stood still. Cherish was also defenseless. She was sitting in her passenger seat. She tried to remain as calm as possible.

The three UFO beings had long, blonde hair, purple-blue eyes and they were tall and slender dressed in long, purple and white robes with golden, sparkling slippers. They appeared attractive and graceful. One of the celestial beings, Tio, spoke to the passengers in the airplane. Tio said, "Don't be alarmed. We come in peace. We come from the Pleiades. We are your cosmic neighbors. We come to warn you that your planet, Earth is in danger. There will be a polar shift soon. Because of this, there will be many changes on the surface of your planet. There will be earthquakes, tidal waves and much flooding. Some continents will sink. We can save you from this destruction by letting you live on our UFO craft. You will be safe here with us. You must accept our help and service if you want to survive."

Cherish heard the words of warning spoken by the celestial beings. She realized these celestial beings had come in peace and they wanted to protect Earthlings from dangers on Earth. She began to relax. She decided to speak to these celestial beings. Cherish said, "I am glad you want to protect us. What planet do you come from?"

The same celestial being, Tio, smiled and responded, "We come from Astaria in the Pleiades. We live in peace and harmony on our planet. You will like our planet. We have perfect weather, pure air and beautiful gardens and waterways. Our people are healthy and happy on Astaria."

Cherish smiled at the three celestial beings. She said, "Your planet sounds like a wonderful place to live." The second celestial being, Sila, said, "We know you will like our planet. Everyone lives in peace." Cherish asked, "Can I see your planet?" This celestial being, Sila, said, "You are welcome to see our planet."

The first celestial being, Tio, spoke to the whole group of passengers, pilots and airline hostesses in the airplane. He said, "You are welcome to step out of this airplane into our craft." The people in the airplane began to relax. Cherish looked at them. She spoke to them. "I know we will be safe and protected here in their craft. They said they live in peace and harmony".

The first celestial being known as Tio said, "Come with us. You will be safe." Cherish followed the three celestial beings. The other passengers, pilots and airline hostesses followed the three celestial beings into the UFO craft. Once they were inside the enormous craft from another planet they walked through a long tubular tunnel made of shining, metallic material.

At the end of the tunnel the three celestial beings, Cherish and everyone else from the airplane stepped into a large room which had light lavender walls and sparkling star like designs glittering on the ceiling and walls. There were geometric couches, chairs and tables that appeared transparent. Large screens were on the walls. Fresh fruit in large bowls were on the tables.

Tio spoke to the Earthlings. He said, "Make yourself comfortable. Here is fresh fruit to refresh you." The Earthlings sat on the couches and chairs near bowls of fruit. They began eating the delicious fruit. Other celestial beings dressed in long white and gold robes with golden sandals served a delicious, cool fruit drink to everyone.

The Earthlings felt welcome, comfortable and nourished by the fresh fruit and fruit drinks. They saw movies on the screens on the walls while they ate and drank. There were films showing what Astaria looked like. They observed gardens, waterways and astro domes in Astarian cities. These movies helped the Earthlings see how beautiful and safe Astaria was.

Tio spoke to the Earthlings again. He said, "You have seen what Astaria looks like. You will be happy and safe there. When we arrive on Astaria you will begin a new and better life. It is important that you live in peace and harmony as we do."

Cherish noticed a celestial male looking at her in a special way. She wondered if he was interested in knowing her. She continued to eat some fruit and sip the delicious nectar. After a while he came over to her and introduced himself to her. He said, "My name is Libro. What is your name?" Cherish replied, "My name is Cherish." Libro continued, "If there is anything you need, let me know." Cherish glanced at Libro, who had red hair, crystal blue eyes, handsome facial features and was tall and slender. She was attracted to him.

Libro sat with Cherish to become acquainted with her. She said, "I hope life on Astaria will be interesting. I have never been on another planet before." Libro replied, "I think you will appreciate Astara for its beauty and climate. It is never too hot or too cold on Astaria. We have plenty to do to keep us busy."

Cherish looked at Libro with an inquisitive expression. She asked, "What do you do to keep busy?" Libro said, "We garden, swim and go to halls of learning to expand our awareness." Cherish asked, "What do you learn at the halls of learning?" Libro said, "We learn about the Master's teachings, about our eternal God of the Cosmic Plan and about our Cosmos".

Cherish was amazed that she was in the presence of a celestial being who she could communicate immediately and intelligently with. She realized his lifestyle was more spiritual and advanced than anyone on Earth. She was fascinated with him. She wanted to know him much better.

Tio, Sila and Cara, the three celestial beings, walked around to become more acquainted with the Earthlings. Other Astarians, who were dressed in white and purple robes, who had blonde or red hair and crystal blue eyes, walked around to become more familiar with the Earthlings.

Time was timeless on the celestial craft. The Earthlings were not aware that they were approaching Astaria. Once the celestial craft landed on Astaria Tio spoke to the Earthlings. Tio said,

"We have landed on Astaria. You must step into a special oxygen chamber before you leave this craft."

The Earthlings wondered why they were asked to enter a special oxygen chamber. Tio continued, "Your lungs must adjust gradually to the oxygen on our planet. We have much purer oxygen than you are accustomed to. Once you are directly in Astaria's atmosphere you will begin to breathe pure air.

The Earthlings were assisted into the special oxygen chamber in another room in the craft. They remained in the chambers for approximately an hour. Then the three, celestial beings led them out of the celestial craft on to Astaria. Astaria was a true paradise with magnificent gardens and waterways like they saw in the films on the celestial craft. Astro domes were in the city.

The Earthlings began a new life on a beautiful, peaceful planet. They were made to feel welcome on Astaria. They were given places to dwell. They went to the halls of learning to learn all they could about Astaria, its way of life and about the Cosmic Plan.

Cherish became good friends with Libro. He showed her around Astaria. They went swimming together and they walked into many gardens. Libro shared his wisdom and knowledge about the Cosmos. He revealed his spiritual insights and truths. Cherish was very happy and healthy. She became peaceful, blissful and much more serene because she had discovered a new life filled with spiritual truth and wisdom.

FORTY-NINE

Meditation

Meditation is a quiet time to look within to become One with God. Prayers and aspirations help uplift our souls. To learn to quiet the outer mind is the way to understanding and listening to the inner voice within.

Each soul can become aware of his or her higher mind. The Christ Self descends into the soul presence to enlighten the mind and soul. The Christ Self awakens the soul to God consciousness.

The art of meditation helps to bring peace within one's soul. White light frees the soul from darkness. White light flows down the spine in the chakra centers to awaken one's soul to truth and wisdom.

Meditation helps a soul to control the lower mind and lower emotions. Illuminated thoughts flow through one's mind to enlighten the soul.

FIFTY

Self Responsibility

Self responsibility is necessary for soul growth. The development of values and moral control are important in order to develop self realization.

Each person has the opportunity to awaken to right action, right concentration, right association, right occupation and right morals.

Every responsibility helps a person become mature. Maturity is developed step by step because a person learns to participate in duties and expectations. For example, children are given chores to do such as dusting, vacuuming, washing dishes, hanging up clothes on clotheslines, weeding the garden, washing the family car and helping to cook and set the dinner table. Children usually have homework after school.

Everyone is responsible to clean his and her body by taking a shower or a bath. One's hair should be washed and styled. Daily combing of one's hair is necessary. Other grooming habits such as cutting, cleaning and filing our fingernails are necessary. We need to wash our teeth and face. Body deodorants are used so we smell fresh. We select certain clothes to wear in order to look our best. We are required to wear clothes.

We are responsible to maintain good health by eating nutritious food. We need to exercise regularly by walking. Daily exposure to the Sun helps to give us Vitamin D. Maintenance of good table manners is expected. Courtesy and proper use of language are important.

A person's character is developed by developing virtues and values throughout one's life. Participating in church activities and other community events helps a person acquire self responsibility. We should create goals and purposes for our lives to promote self responsibility.

— FIFTY-ONE —

Tupperware

Tupperware is made out of plastic. Many kinds of containers are made to use for storing food in the kitchen. Vegetables and fruits as well as leftovers from meals are stored in Tupperware containers.

Tupperware containers have lids to seal food. Food lasts longer in these containers. Tupperware doesn't break because it is made of plastic. Many sizes are used so that they can fit in the refrigerator and shelves. Food is sealed from bacteria and air in Tupperware with lids.

Tupperware parties are given at different peoples' homes. Tupperware is displayed. People select different Tupperware. They may order a certain amount and type of Tupperware. It is easy to store Tupperware in one's kitchen.

Tupperware can be easily carried to potlucks with sealed food. You can purchase Tupperware at Tupperware parties, department stores, at Dollar Tree, Rite Aid, Wal Marts and K Marts. Tupperware can be ordered from catalogues. The Tupperware is shipped or mailed to you.

Tupperware has become a valuable household product. You can save food and money by using Tupperware regularly.

FIFTY-TWO

Making Decorations

Making decorations is a creative experience. Decorations are made for special events, parties and holidays. Specific materials are needed to create certain decorations.

Decorations made for parties are made out of colorful paper. Hanging objects and long strings of designs around a room add to the décor for birthday parties, weddings and community events. Large, painted mosaics and murals are interesting to display in the room.

Christmas celebrations and parties are festive. It is a time to decorate Christmas trees with lights, colorful bulbs, stars and other paper objects that hang on the tree. Displays of the Bethlehem scene add to the setting. Christmas stockings are hung on the fireplace mantle. Pictures and statuettes of Santa Claus may be displayed around the living room.

Many people decorate their front yards with Christmas trees which are decorated. Santa's sleigh and reindeer may be displayed. The Bethlehem scene is often displayed.

Children and adults make decorations for Halloween, Easter and Thanksgiving. Children make black cats, pumpkins, ghosts, witches and owls out of colored paper to display on walls. Bulletin board decorations add to the classroom décor.

Easter eggs are painted with different colors and designs. Easter bunnies and rabbit decorations are displayed. Paper designs of Easter eggs and flowers are made and displayed. Thanksgiving paper turkeys are made to display. Fruit and pumpkins are displayed on dinner tables for Thanksgiving.

People make decorations for Christmas, Easter, Thanksgiving and New Year's parades. Colored paper, scissors, tape, glue, confetti, miniature objects and plastic objects are used to make decorations.

FIFTY-THREE

Ways To Use Paper

Paper can be used to write on 8 ½" by 11" and blank paper is used for typing and writing on. Colored paper is used for cut-outs to make decorations. Many designs can be made by using scissors to cut them out.

Paper Mache is fun to create. Newspapers are glued on balloons. The paper Mache objects are painted different colors. Cut, paper strips may be glued on the paper Mache objects.

Paper hats can be made by shaping, folding and creasing paper. Party hats are made out of paper. Kites are made out of paper and held together with thin, wood framing. There are many types of kites made out of paper.

Large sheets of butcher and bulletin board paper are used to make murals and bulletin board displays. Paper borders are stapled around the edges of the rectangular or square bulletin boards.

Paper is used to make paper cups, paper glasses, paper plates and paper napkins. Paper is lightweight and easy to carry places and to store away. Those kitchen materials are disposable once they are used.

Notebooks, folders, envelopes, stationery, cards, pamphlets, books, magazines and newspapers are made out of paper. Sheet music, art paper and journals are made with paper. Some clothes such as aprons and dresses are made with paper.

Paper is very useful because it can be used for many purposes. Paper is produced from wood pulp from trees. Paper has been produced for many years.

FIFTY-FOUR

Remedies For Diseases

Remedies have been found to prevent diseases and to cure diseases. The common cold can be treated with Vitamin C, medicinal throat rinses, lozenges and nutritious food. Medications are prescribed by doctors such as antibiotics to kill harmful germs.

Flu can be cured with antibiotics, fruit juices and other flu medications. Pneumonia must be treated with special antibiotics. Avoid mingling near people who are stricken with flu and colds. Sore throats can be cured with throat rinses and antibiotic sprays.

Leukemia may be cured by cleaning blood vessels and by increasing blood cells to counteract white blood cells. Anemia may contribute to leukemia. Iron and magnesium can cure the blood stream. A proper diet of fresh fruits, vegetables and amino acids will help to prevent leukemia and many other diseases.

Contagious diseases are usually difficult to stop. Sterilize cooking equipment, dishes, cups, glasses and silverware before using them. Sterilize door knobs. Open windows to air out your house. Keep your toilets, sinks, floors and furniture clean. Unnecessary, harmful germs can be avoided.

Maintain a consistent, nutritious diet. Avoid drinking sodas, coffee, white flour, white sugar, grease and old leftovers and overripe fruit and vegetables. Eat in moderation and eat a variety of nutritious foods which are fresh. In this way you will strengthen your immune system. Avoid unnecessary and harmful drugs. You can prevent diseases if you maintain good health.

─── FIFTY-FIVE ───

Foster Parents

Couples adopt babies, young children and even teenagers. Adopted children live with foster parents. Foster parents are given birth certificates for their adopted children. These adopted children live with their foster parents.

Mary Lou Kincaid and Joseph Kincaid tried to have children of their own. They waited ten years hoping to give birth to a baby boy or girl. They were unable to have their own children. They lived in Detroit, Michigan.

So, the Kincaids decided to adopt children. They went to an Adoption Agency in their regional area to request to adopt a baby. They were anxious to become parents. When they were interviewed at the Hopkins Adoption Agency in their vicinity the interviewer, Sara Adams, asked Mary Lou and Joseph Kincaid questions. The interviewer asked, "Why do you want to adopt a baby?" Mary Lou replied, "We want to be parents. We tried to have our own children first." Joseph commented, "We love children. So, we want to adopt a baby."

The interviewer, Sara Adams, asked, "Are you working and earning a sufficient income?" Joseph Kincaid responded. "I am a business manager at a large business firm in Detroit." Sara Adams asked, "Do you have a bedroom for a baby?" Mary Lou answered, "We live in a three bedroom house. We can fix up a nursery in one of the bedrooms. We have a crib already." Sara Adams said, "Please fill out these adoption papers. We have a baby girl who needs a home. Once we have processed these forms I will contact you. "She handed the Kincaids the adoption papers to fill out.

Mary Lou and Joseph smiled. Joseph said, "Thank you. When can we see the baby girl? Sara Adams replied, "As soon as the adoption forms are filled out, cleared and processed I will call you. You will be able to come back to the adoption agency to see the baby." Mary Lou asked, "What is the baby's name?" Sara Adams answered, "Her name is Jennifer." Mary Lou looked happy. She hoped to see the baby soon.

The Kincaids thanked Sara Adams. Then they left the adoption agency. They waited to hear from her after they filled out the adoption papers and returned them to the agency. Sara Adams called the Kincaids

two weeks later. Mary Lou and Joseph came back to the adoption agency to see the baby girl.

Sara Adams brought the baby girl into her office to show the Kincaids. This baby girl was 6 months old. She had red hair, blue eyes and she was Caucasian. She was healthy looking. Mary Lou and Joseph gazed at the baby girl. Mary Lou smiled and said, She is beautiful. May I hold her?" Sara handed Jennifer to Mary Lou. Mary Lou cuddled the baby. Jennifer responded to Mary Lou's attention. Joseph stood near Mary Lou. He held the baby's hand. He touched her face gently.

Sara Adams said, "The adoption paperwork has been cleared and processed. You can take Jennifer home with you." Mary Lou radiated with happiness. Joseph was very pleased that Mary Lou and he had been accepted at the adoption agency. Joseph said, "We will take good care of the baby. She is adorable."

Sara Adams handed Mary Lou a pink blanket to wrap around Jennifer. Sara said, "I will be coming by to visit you soon." Mary Lou replied, "Let us know when you are coming over. We want to be sure to be home." Sara smiled and remarked. "I will call you to inform you when I am coming over to see your home and baby nursery." Mary Lou and Joseph thanked Sara Adams for helping them receive a baby.

When Mary Lou and Joseph went to their home they brought their adopted daughter, Jennifer into their house. They allowed her to crawl on the living room floor so she could exercise. Jennifer crawled around and touched some chairs and a couch. She explored the corners of the living room. She was dressed in diapers with a comfortable jumper on.

Joseph went to the nearby grocery store to buy Simalac fortified milk and baby food in small jars. Mary Lou had given her husband a list of things to purchase for Jennifer. Mary Lou had a list of baby foods, comfortable play clothes for a 6 months old baby and some baby shoes.

Mary Lou had already purchased baby blankets, hanging mobiles and baby toys which were already put in the nursery bedroom. Mary Lou took Jennifer into her nursery and she put her in the crib. She stood near the crib and moved the hanging mobile so Jennifer could enjoy looking at it. Jennifer looked at the bright colors and shapes over her head. Jennifer reached her hand up to the moving mobiles. Jennifer stood up in the crib. She held onto the crib sides so she could remain standing. She finally touched the moving mobiles. She appeared fascinated with the colorful, moving shapes. Mary Lou watched Jennifer playing with the hanging mobiles. She enjoyed observing Jennifer.

Joseph came home with Simalac formula, baby food, packages of diapers, baby clothes and more toys. He brought these items into the house. Joseph laid the packages and bags of purchased things in the kitchen. He went into the nursery to see Jennifer and his wife, Mary Lou. Joseph saw Jennifer hold onto the sides of her crib. He noticed she was playing with the colorful mobiles.

Joseph placed some new toys made of plastic and stuffed cotton in Jennifer's crib. Jennifer went over to touch the new toys. She began playing with the new toys. Joseph and Mary Lou watched their adopted daughter playing in her crib.

Mary Lou told Joseph that she needed to prepare Jennifer's milk and baby food. Mary Lou left the nursery and went into the kitchen to prepare Jennifer's food. She warmed up some Similac in a bottle. She tested the formula to be sure it wasn't too hot or too cold. She opened some cream corn, mashed string beans and custard pudding.

Mary Lou walked back into the nursery. She picked Jennifer up and took her into the kitchen. She placed Jennifer in her new high chair. Mary Lou put a bib on Jennifer to cover her jumper. Mary Lou picked up a baby spoon. She started feeding Jennifer the creamed corn; then the string beans and then the custard pudding. Jennifer ate all the soft food. Then Mary Lou brought Jennifer back to her crib. She laid Jennifer down. She placed the baby bottle in Jennifer's mouth. Jennifer began sucking up the Simalac formula. Mary Lou turned on soft, relaxing music. Jennifer drank all the Simalac formula from the baby bottle. Jennifer became drowsy. She fell asleep within five minutes.

Mary Lou and Joseph were pleased how the first day transpired. Jennifer responded well in her new home. She seemed to be an adaptable baby. During the night Jennifer woke up. She was wet and hungry at 2 a.m. Mary Lou heard her crying. Mary Lou came into her new daughter's room.

Jennifer was still crying because she was uncomfortable and hungry. Mary Lou changed her diaper first and made sure her crib was dry. She prepared another clean baby bottle with Simalac formula. Mary Lou laid Jennifer down in her crib and placed the luke warm baby bottle in her mouth. Jennifer had stopped crying. She began sucking the milk. She calmed down and finished the formula. Mary Lou decided to sing some songs to her to relax her. Finally, Jennifer fell asleep again.

Mary Lou went back to her bedroom to rest in bed with her husband. She was tired. She fell asleep. At 6:15 a.m. she heard Jennifer crying again. So, Mary Lou got up and went into check on Jennifer. Jennifer was still crying. So, Mary Lou picked her new daughter up and cuddled her. She took her into the kitchen. She warmed up soft oatmeal, mashed banana and prepared Simalac formula.

Mary Lou placed her daughter in her high chair. She fed Jennifer the oatmeal, bananas and milk formula. Jennifer ate up all the food and drank the formula. After she was done eating Mary Lou cleaned Jennifer up, changed her diaper and she put clean clothes on Jennifer.

Jennifer was allowed to crawl on the kitchen floor. She crawled into the living room. Mary Lou put some toys on the living room floor for Jennifer to play with. Mary Lou kept an eye on Jennifer to be sure she was safe while she played.

Mary Lou thought about her role as a mother. She hoped to be a good and loving mother. She remembered how her parents raised her. Mary Lou had devoted parents. Mary Lou intended to raise her daughter with love, wisdom and truth.

Joseph woke up and came into the living room around 7:15 a.m. He was in his bathrobe. He saw his adopted daughter playing on the living room carpet. He picked her up and hugged her. He played with her. He was glad to be a father at last. Mary Lou and Joseph looked after their adopted daughter. They taught her to walk and talk.

Jennifer continued to grow day by day, week by week and month by month. She went through the usual stages of development. She remained healthy, alert and she was a happy child because she was loved and cared for by her foster parents.

FIFTY-SIX

Extravaganzas

An extravaganza is a special celebration where a festival takes place. Many people gather together to sing, dance and eat a variety of tasty food. Bands play and vocal soloists perform. A parade may take place with many participants who line up and walk down the main street.

Several extravaganzas take place in Santa Barbara, San Diego and San Francisco. Each celebration is planned long before the events take place. Costumes are designed. Menus for festive foods are carefully planned well in advance. The main streets are decorated with flowers and garlands. Festive music is played with guitars, banjos and castanets. Extravaganzas are happy times where people celebrate.

─── FIFTY-SEVEN ───

Destinations Into Outerspace

Many destinations into outer space have occurred. NASA in America has launched flights to the Moon, to Venus, Mars and Jupiter. Photographs and films have been taken showing the surface of Venus, Mars, the Moon, Jupiter, Saturn and Moons revolving around Jupiter such as Europa.

Destinations into outer space have made a difference because humanity has been expanding their awareness about our solar system and our galaxy. Each flight into outer space provides astronauts with knowledge and awareness of life and conditions in outer space.

Scientists, astronomers and astronauts have learned that there is much space between Suns, planets, galaxies and nebula. The laws of centralization, polar opposites, gravitation and magnetism affect the balance and equilibrium in outer space. Gravitation keeps the planets revolving around the Sun. Magnetism and gravitation holds objects on the surface of planets. Gravitational pull varies on each planet, planetoid and Moon. The Sun holds planets in a cyclic revolution as they travel around the Sun in their specific orbit.

Outer space is vast and there is much for humanity to learn about its mysteries and dimensions. Scientists and astronomers continue to find out more about outer space. There is much to learn about the cosmos.

FIFTY EIGHT

Moments Of Ecstasy

Moments of ecstasy enhance our lives. The joy of awakening to interdimensions expands and uplifts our souls. We awaken to a deeper purpose for life. We surround ourselves with beautiful things. We are uplifted when we meditate and look within.

Moments of ecstasy come and go. These rare moments awaken us to dimensions we have not understood before. The interdimensions are on other planes which are more refined. We can see into higher realms eventually with our inner eye if we pursue this opportunity.

To observe a crystal, shining light ray blazing nearby is spectacular. Dazzling, diamond light sparkles across the ocean because of bright Sunlight beaming in the water. Sunrises and sunsets blaze with brilliant, vivid colors of red, pink, yellow, purple and orange.

The magic of Spring is refreshing to the spirit. Many colorful flowers blossom in the Spring. Baby birds chirp in nests. Squirrels climb up and down trees. New grass and wild lupins, pink ladies and poppies can be seen everywhere. These fragrant, wild flowers purify the air.

Falling in love with someone special is a wonderful feeling of ecstasy. Loving someone for his or her fine character and qualities is worthwhile. Affection and warmth add to a loving relationship with the opposite sex.

Moments of ecstasy may suddenly come and go. We should appreciate these special moments when they happen.

FIFTY-NINE

Dressing Up

Dressing up is usually done when we go to formal occasions such as weddings, parties, ballroom dancing, to the opera and stage play theater and to special ceremonies. People dress up for leadership positions, administrative jobs, for parades and celebrations.

The bride and groom, best man, bridesmaids and matron dress up. The bride usually wears a fancy, long, white dress. She wears a veil and she may wear flowers or a decorative hat. The white dress may have sequins, beads and small pearls sewn on her wedding dress. The groom, best man and Pall Bearers wear a formal, black or blue suit with a vest and ties. They wear black, leather shoes.

Bridesmaids and the matron of honor wear long pastel, colored dresses and flowers in their hair. The bride and groom's parents dress up for the wedding. The mothers wear fancy dresses or suits, with hats and high heels or other dress shoes. The fathers wear formal suits, ties and leather shoes.

High school proms are formal occasions. Girls dress up in formal gowns and fancy shoes. They fix up their hair. Boys wear suits and formal, leather shoes and ties. Girls usually wear corsages if they are escorted by a date to the prom.

People even dress up for funerals. They wear formal dresses, pants suits and attractive shoes. People dress up in costumes for different parades and celebrations in their community. People dress up for holiday events.

Churchgoers usually dress up to go to church. Women wear their best dress or pants suit to church with formal shoes and gloves. Men dress up in suits or sports suits and dress shoes.

Girls and boys dress up in their best clothes for school parties, birthday parties and other parties. Dressing up is fun and appropriate for formal and special occasions.

———— SIXTY ————

Learning About Scandinavia

Traveling to Scandinavia in Northern Europe is a special experience. Scandinavian countries are Denmark, Norway, Sweden, Finland and Iceland.

Water is the most important resource for generating electricity in Norway, Iceland and Sweden, where fast flowing rivers have encouraged the building of hydroelectric power stations. In Norway, hydroelectric power meets 99.8 percent of electricity and the percentage is almost the same in Iceland and Sweden. Sweden also depends on nuclear energy. Finland also gets much of its supply from nuclear reactors. Denmark relies mostly on imported coal and oil to produce its electricity.

Denmark, Finland, Iceland, Norway and Sweden were once united under a single crown. Denmark, Finland, Iceland, Norway and Sweden are five nations linked by religious, historical and geographical ties. The functional integration within the frontiers of Scandinavia is unique in the world. Under the terms of the 1962 Helsinki Treaty, these five Nordic states, who prefer the term "Norden" to describe their presence, to maintain and develop cooperation in legal, cultural, social and economic fields. They have a common postage rate and increasingly, progressive industrial, commercial, legal and educational system.

Scandinavia has a common labor market and a common passport area, being integrated to such a degree that Danes, Finns, Icelanders, Norwegians and Swedes enjoy a remarkable degree of mutual citizenship. They have almost as much freedom of movement and settlement as Americans have within the 50 states of the United States.

Sweden switched to driving on the right-hand side of the road on September 3, 1967, which is called H-Day. H means right. They conformed with the neighboring Nordic countries. Nordic conformity is extraordinary because Scandinavia's 22.5 million inhabitants are scattered far and wide over lands separated by the Baltic Sea, the North Sea and the Atlantic Ocean.

Iceland is the most isolated country in Europe. It lies 900 kilometers from the peninsula of Norway and Sweden. Scandinavia has a land area of 1,257,284 square kilometers, greater than Britain, France and West Germany combined. All Scandinavian countries are high-latitude lands on the northwest fringes of Europe. All of them experience high costs in maintaining their communications systems because of the nature of their topography. All five countries possess a limited variety of natural resources. Timber is abundant in Finland and Sweden and both have vast wilderness areas.

The five Nordic countries were first united in 1397 when Queen Margrethe of Denmark established the Union of Kalmar, joining Denmark, Norway and Sweden as well as Iceland and

Finland under one crown. The union ended officially with the secession of Sweden in 1523. However, Norway, Denmark, Iceland, and the Faeroe Islands remained united for several centuries under a single monarchy. Finland had six and a half centuries of close association with Sweden before being ceded to Russia in 1809 and becoming a Grand Duchy.

The five Scandinavian countries are now urbanized and they have modern industrial and service economies. All of them have egalitarian societies, advanced social security systems and very high living standards. Denmark, Norway and Sweden are constitutional monarchies; whereas both Iceland and Finland have an elected president as their head of state. Fundamentally, all the countries are Western-style, parliamentary democracies that are governed by representation. All of them have so many well supported political parties so that coalition governments prevail.

Scandinavians are 95 percent in the Lutheran religion. Finland is officially bilingual. Most Finns understand their second language which is Swedish. Scandinavians have established a Nordic Council, an organization set up by Norway, Sweden, Denmark and Iceland for co-operation between their governments. Finland became a member in 1955. Denmark's Atlantic outposts, Greenland and the Faeroe Islands, together with the Aland Islands, have been granted the right to nominate their own representatives.

The first significant achievements of the Nordic Council came in 1954 when the member Scandinavian countries agreed to a common labor market, which enabled their nationals to work and settle in any of the signatory lands without a work permit or a permanent resident's visa. Since then, more than one million persons have migrated from one Nordic country to another. Many migrants came from Finland to Sweden.

FINLAND

Finland is an unusual country in an unusual place. Finland is surrounded by ice and water. The Finns define themselves with the word sisu. Sisu means courage, stubbornness, endurance, strength, determination and pride. Finns use this word to talk about their character and their ability to face and conquer challenges.

The Finnish people have faced many challenges. They fought in terrible wars. They have found themselves in the middle of tense international conflicts. They have weathered economic depression and rapidly changing industries. Sisu gave the Finns the courage to survive the devastation of World War II and sisu inspires Finnish athletes to play harder and go faster. Sisu produces new businesses in Finland.

Talkaut is another important word which means "community work." Talkaut means to help a friend move to a new apartment or it could involve an organization such as a church group painting the walls of a local school. Talkaut means cooperation and responsibility. This spirit of cooperation is evident in Finland's generous social programs and opportunities for all. Finns take their freedom and democracy seriously. They work hard to make things right for their people and their environment.

Finns are fun loving people. Many Finns love the outdoors. They ski, run and ride bicycles. They make beautiful ceramics and textiles. They have joyous celebrations. They work hard and they play hard. Racing with reindeers is popular in Finland.

Finland is a country of wildflowers, berries, and rugged coastlines perfect for fishing. There are thousands of lakes and islands. You can witness the northern lights. Finland shares borders with Norway to the north, Sweden to the northwest and Russia to the east. The Baltic Sea lies to the south and southwest. The arm of the Baltic along Finland's west coast is called the Gulf of Bothnia, while the part of the Baltic to Finland's south is called the Gulf of Finland.

Finland has about 775 miles of coastline and more than eighty thousand small islands in the Baltic Sea. The Finnish coastline constantly changes as more land rises up from the sea. It is estimated that Finland gains about 2 square miles a year.

Helsinki sits by the Gulf of Finland. Several islands lie offshore. The Baltic Sea wraps around much of Finland. The Finnish people and economy depend on it. The five Scandinavian countries signed an agreement at a Helsinki Convention in 1974. This agreement tries to protect the Baltic Sea. The nations that border the Baltic hope to completely restore the sea's environment by 2021.

Finland lies atop granite, a type of volcanic rock. The granite beneath Finland is about 1.5 billion years old. Glaciers have scraped away at the land over millions of years, leaving the rock exposed. The Finns value rock as an important natural resource. At many quarries, they cut granite or limestone from the ground. They remove copper and zinc from the rock.

Finland has territory above the Arctic Circle. Finland experiences the midnight Sun. The Sun never sets in parts of Finland during the summer. During the winter the North Pole points away from the Sun throughout the day, and the Sun never rises in some parts of Finland which is called the polar night.

Finns in northern reaches of the country live without the Sun for about fifty days a year. On the shortest day of the year, December 21, the Sun shines for only six hours in Helsinki.

One of the splendors of Finland occurs during the long winter nights. The sky lights up with brilliant bursts of colored lights, known as the aurora borealis or northern lights. It is caused by charged particles from the Sun hitting the earth's atmosphere. In northern Finland, the aurora borealis appears as many as two hundred times a year. In southern Finland it may be visible only fifteen times a year.

In Finnish, the auroras are called revontulet, which means "fox fires." The Finns have a folktale about an arctic fox starting fires with its tail. It shot sparks into the sky, forming the auroras. The Sami people, who live in the northern part of Finland, known as Lapland, believed that people should remain silent when witnessing the lights. Praise or criticism could anger the lights, inciting them to kill their views.

Finland is divided into several regions, each with its own character and climate. Most Finns live in the coastal lowlands which are between 40 and 80 miles wide which hugs the coast along the Baltic Sea from Sweden to Russia. The major cities of Helsinki, Espoo and Turku are in this region. The coastal lowlands are flat, with few forests and easy access to the sea. Rivers flow through the coastal lowlands to the Baltic Sea, making it easy for boats to travel through the region.

Finland's best agricultural land is in the coastal lowlands and most of Finland's seventy thousand farms are found there. Farmers in Finland grow mainly grains, such as barley, oats, wheat, potatoes and rye.

Finland has more than 180,000 small islands, mostly scattered in the Baltic. Some islands called skerries, are too small even to build a house on. About twenty-five thousand people live on the Aland Islands, which lie in the Baltic Sea between Sweden and Finland, off the coast of Turku.

The Aland Islands belong to Finland which is a self governing region with their own parliament. The islands have a mild climate that supports a long growing season.

Finland is a land of lakes. This country has about 190,000 lakes of all sizes. The lakes formed about ten thousand years ago during the Ice Age. Slow moving glaciers gouged lake beds out of the granite. As the Earth warmed and the land rose, the glaciers melted, their water filling the beds to create lakes. Most of Finland's lakes are in the Lake District, which spreads across the southeast of the country. The district is physically separated from the coastal lowlands by the Salpausselka ridges.

The largest lake in Finland is Lake Saimaa, which covers more than 680 square miles. This lake is linked to Vyborg, Russia, by the 35 mile Saimaa Canal, which opened in 1856. The canal is a major transportation route through the area. A number of smaller canals and smaller lakes link to form one large waterway. Lake Payanne, the second largest lake in Finland, drains south into the Gulf of Finland, drains south into the Gulf of Finland by the Kymi River. Houseboats line the shoreline of Lake Saimaa in the summer months.

The Lake District is important in the lives of Finns, even those who don't live there. Many Finns own or rent vacation homes in the district and families flock there in the summertime.

In winter the shallow lakes and waterways freeze and the Finns can go skating, sledding, skiing and ice fishing.

The northernmost part of Finland, called Lapland, lies in the Arctic Circle. This region is mostly high plateaus, lakes and swampland. Finland's highest mountain is in Lapland called Mount Haltia, which reaches 4,356 feet. It is part of a small ridge of mountains that borders Sweden and Norway.

Lapland is where reindeer come from. It is the traditional home of the Sami people. For thousands of years they lived in the far north, herding reindeer and hunting. A few Sami continue to live this way.

Even though Finland is in the Arctic Circle region it is not as cold as some other northerly regions. The Gulf Stream is a powerful ocean current that carries warm water from the Gulf of Mexico north to the Baltic Sea. Southern Finland, where most Finns live, has a northern temperate climate, the same as the northern United States and southern Canada. Winters are long and cold, with temperatures rarely rising above freezing. In Lapland, temperatures sometimes drop below -58 degrees Fahrenheit (-50 degrees Celsius).

Winter begins early in the far north of the country---around mid-October---and slowly creeps south until it reaches the southernmost islands in December. Snow begins to fall in November. It quickly covers the ground and does not melt until April or May. Winter lasts about one hundred days in the southernmost part of Finland and about two hundred days in Lapland.

Helsinki is Finland's capital and largest city with 564,521 residents. Espoo is Finland's second largest city. Vantoo is the fourth largest city in Finland. Both cities are near Helsinki and are considered part of the Helsinki metropolitan area. The population of Espoo has increased tenfold since the mid-twentieth century. Espoo is now home to many science and technology companies.

Tampere is Finland's third largest city, which is an inland city. Tampere began as a market town during the 1700s. By the mid-1800s, it had grown into an industrial powerhouse. This city's factories produced huge quantities of metal and textiles. Most of these factories are now gone. Today, the people of Tampere work in telecommunications and other technology industries.

Turku, the nation's fifth largest city, lies on the southwestern coast. It is the oldest city in Finland and it once was the capital. This city was founded in the 1200s. Soon, a castle and a cathedral were built and this city became the center of medieval Finland. Today, it is a major port city, an education center and the home of thriving high-tech industries. This city has many museums which include the Turku Art Museum and the Turku Castle and Historical Museum.

Spring is a short season in Finland, lasting only about fifty days. Spring begins in early April and reaches Lapland in early May. The lakes in Finland's interior are usually melted in May and June. Summer begins in late May and has reached all parts of Finland by late June. The average high in Helsinki in July is a pleasant 72 degrees F (22 degrees C). In the middle of this country the temperature soars to 95 degrees F (35 C). It rains many summer afternoons. This rain combines with long days and warm Sun to give plants a chance to thrive during their short growing season.

Autumn begins around the last week of August in northern Finland and takes a month to reach the southern islands. Trees cover more than two-thirds of the country of Finland. Lakes and rivers cover about one-tenth of the country. The Baltic Sea makes up almost half of Finland's border. Nature is important economically, historically and culturally to Finland.

Birch trees grow as far north as Urho Kekkonen National Park in Lapland. They are easily identified by their white trunks. Much of Finland is coniferous, or cone-bearing forests. Spruce trees are most common in the south of the country and pine trees are more common in the north. The southern part of Finland has a zone of deciduous trees which include birch, hazel, aspen, maple, elm, linden and alder. Trees are Finland's most valuable, natural resource. Finland is a leading producer of wood and wood products.

Finland is home to eight hundred different mosses and more than one thousand kinds of lichen. All of these have adapted to live in Finland's cold climate. Many native plants of Finland are edible such as lingo berries, cowberries, blueberries and thimbleberries which grow everywhere. Many kinds of mushrooms grow in Finland. Finn's gather mushrooms and berries.

Finland has many wild animals. There are 60 species of mammals and 450 kinds of birds, 70 kinds of fish and a handful of reptiles and amphibians in Finland. Finland is home to all four of Europe's largest predators known as the brown bear, the wolf, wolverines and the lynx. These animals have been hunted for years, but strong conservation efforts are keeping their numbers stable and allowing them to thrive. Other mammals in Finland include reindeers, elk, red foxes, mountain hares, otters and seals.

Finland's animals have adapted to the rough winters. Some, like hares and foxes grow thick fur in winter. Squirrels and arctic foxes change their coloring. The Arctic fox grows a white coat, which causes it to blend in with the snow, making it a better hunter. The squirrel turns the same gray as the branches of the trees it lives in, helping it hide from predators. Other animals and many birds dig burrows in the snow to stay warm.

Finland's forests and coasts attract a large variety of birds. Hazel hens, grouse, white tailed eagles and ptarmigans live in the forest. At least ten species of owls live in the country, which include the pygmy owl and the Tengmalm's owl. The whooper swan and crane live in Finland. Arctic birds include elder ducks and guillemots fly-over Finland. Thousands of acres of Finnish land have been set aside as nature preserves for migrating birds. Humans are not allowed in most of these areas during busy migration times.

In Finland, many animals, including bears, hedgehogs, badgers and bats, hibernate in the winter. They spend the winter sleeping in caves, dens or other safe places. Once the ice thaws and berries, leaves and other foods begin to reappear, the animals wake up and head back into the world to eat and move around.

In Finland, the bear is called the king of the forest and is important in folk stories and songs. The whooper swan was sacred to many of the ancient people of Finland. Finland's most common fish is the perch. In Finland, birch has been used to make everything from fires to baskets. Finns make a drink from birch sap. Lily-of-the-Valley is a wildflower which grows all over Finland. It has a strong scent. Finland has thirty-five national parks.

The people in Finland are Swedish-speaking Finns known as Finland Swedes, the Sami people and Romanies (Gypsies). Most Finns have blonde hair. The Sami culture was tied to nature and the people lived close to the land. Today approximately 6,500 Sami in Finland live modern lives and hold different kinds of jobs. Finnish laws protect Sami culture. In 1996, the Sami Parliament was established. The parliament has twenty-one members. Today, there are Sami-language newspapers, radio broadcasts and television shows.

The Romany people are an ethnic group that is spread across Europe and around the world. Romanies were traditional nomadic, moving from place to place. They arrived in Finland in the 1500s. Today, Finland is home to about ten thousand Romanies, most of whom live in or near Helsinki. Romanies in Finland tend to have more trouble finding jobs than other Finns and their housing is often poor. Many Romanies continue to wear their traditional dress---large skirts for women and dark suits for men.

The number of immigrants in Finland has been low. In 1980, only 12,800 foreigners lived in Finland. Most were from Sweden, Germany, the United States and the Soviet Union. By 1990, the number of foreigners living in Finland has risen to 26,000. Most were Swedes. As of 2002, 152,000 foreigners lived in Finland. Russians are now the largest immigrant group, followed by Estonians, Swedes and Samalis. The first Samalis came to Finland in 1991 as political refugees.

Finland prides itself on its excellent education system. Finnish school children usually score among the highest in the world in reading, math and science tests. Children learn math, history, geography, literature, civics, environmental science, music, art, physical education and at last three languages---Finnish, Swedish and English. A single classroom teacher teaches most of the subjects. This basic schooling is called comprehensive school.

Once teenagers complete comprehensive school they have a choice ---vocational school or secondary school. Vocational programs last for two to five years and train students for jobs in the workforce. Secondary school, which lasts three years, prepares students to go to college. Entrance to Finnish universities is competitive. Finland's largest university is the University of Helsinki. Finns credit their education system for their strong economy and high standard of living.

SWEDEN

Sweden is another Scandinavian country in the Arctic Circle. About half of Sweden's boundaries are in the water---the Baltic Sea on the east and the North Sea on the southwest. The coastline is 4,720 miles. The Swedish people are well known as seafarers.

There are 90,000 to 100,000 lakes in Sweden. There are 20,600 miles of rivers. Most of the rivers are not usable for transportation. However, they are a valuable natural resource. Sweden is a long, narrow country. It is the fifth largest, European nation. Only Russia, Ukraine, France and Spain are larger.

North of the Baltic Sea, a short part of the eastern boundary is shared with Finland and Norway, which are next-door neighbors on the west. The Baltic Straits separate Sweden from Denmark.

Sweden and Norway make up the Scandinavian Peninsula. Denmark was once connected to that land.

Southern Sweden, Gotaland, has two types of terrain, the lowlands and highlands. Skane (Scandia), has forests and fertile valleys and plains. It is the best agricultural region of Sweden. The land is similar to the area in Denmark and northern Germany that was once connected to it.

The coastal cities of Skane were important trading ports during the Middle Ages. Some of the traders grew very rich and they built mansions in the region. More than 200 castles and huge homes remain. Smaland, has an irregular rocky coastline on the Baltic Sea. There are many bays and inlets, white cliffs and sandy beaches. Rough, low islands lie offshore. One of them, Oland, is 85 miles long. There is a lighthouse on the island of Oland.

Goteborg is Scandinavia's largest port and the tenth largest in Europe. Goteberg is Sweden's second largest city. Goteberg grew out of a Viking settlement in the eleventh century. In 1621 King Gutav II Adolph granted Goteborg a charter to establish a free trade port. This city is located on both banks of the Gota River. The Volvo, famous automobile manufacturer, comes from Goteberg. In 1995, Goteborg had an estimated population of 444,553.

Malmo is the capital of the province of Skane and is Sweden's third largest city. The name Malmo means sand mounds. Malmo was under Danish rule until 1658. Textile manufacturing, food processing and shipbuilding are some of Malmo's industries.

Uppsala is Sweden's principal university town. Viking ceremonies continued to be performed into the eleventh century even after the introduction of Christianity into Sweden. Uppsala University was established in 1477 by Archbishop Jakob Ulfson. This university remained the main function of Uppsala for centuries. Uppsala lies along both banks of the Fyris River.

Stockholm is Sweden's capital city. It is the largest city in Sweden and Stockholm lies on fourteen small islands on Malarono at Lake Malar, which empties into the Baltic Sea. In 1252 Birger Jarl built a fortified castle and the surrounding city. He is the founder of Stockholm, even though there were settlers from an earlier date. There is a medieval city called Gamla Stan (Old Town) nestled within modern Stockholm.

Democracy has existed in Sweden since Viking days. Four groups were the nobles, clergy, burghers and peasants represented in the Riksdag during the Middle Ages. About 150 years ago two houses of government were formed. The constitution of 1975 changed the Riksdag to a unicameral (one house) parliament, elected by the people. It is responsible for passing laws and for selecting leaders to run the nineteen departments of the government.

The Riksdag is in session from October to May each year. One of its first duties after an election is to select a prime minister. Usually the prime minister is selected because of winning the most votes. Elections to seats in the parliament are normally held every three years. All citizens aged eighteen or over can vote. Citizens of other nations who have lived in Sweden for three years can vote in local, but no national elections.

The Rikadag has 349 members. Most of them represent geographic districts or constituencies. Thirty-nine of the members are chosen differently. These seats are distributed among the various political parties, in proportion to the total number of votes cast for each party.

Sweden has five major political parties and several minor ones. The major parties are the Center, Moderate, Liberal, Social Democrats and Greens, (an environmental party). Since the late 1920s, the Social Democrats have been the party most often in power.

Swedish people take voting seriously. At least 90 percent of eligible voters go to the polls. Sweden's court system consists of a Supreme Court, Supreme Administrative Court, Labor Court, District Courts and Courts of Appeal.

Sweden is divided into counties and municipalities for local government purposes. As of 1995 there were 288 municipal governments and 23 county council areas. The central government appoints county governors. Local councils are elected by the people on the same day as national elections.

Local governments are responsible for collecting taxes. They also supervise the administration of national programs. These include education, public transportation and health care. Sweden is sometimes admired among nations for having found a "middle way" between capitalism and socialism. Very few Swedish industries are nationalized and private enterprise thrives. The Social Democratic Party has not tried to take an active role in industry. It concentrates on providing social benefits for the citizens.

The Swedish people believe that all citizens are entitled to a certain standard of living. This includes guaranteed medical and dental care, pensions, education and many other services. People who cannot work because of sickness, injury, or unemployment receive allowances. In spite of high taxes to pay for these benefits, the general standard of living in Sweden is one of the highest in the world.

Glasswork factories in Smaland are famous for their fine products. On the west coast is Goteberg, one of Sweden's three largest cities. The other two are Malmo, in Skane and Stockholm, the capital of Sweden. The southern uplands have poorer soils and a cooler, wetter climate than the lowlands. Hills in the north slope steeply down to plains. There are patches of peat bogs and day deposits. Two-thirds of the land is in forest, with a rich mixture of deciduous (leafy) and coniferous (cone-bearing) trees.

Regular checkerboard patterns to the towns and farms of southern Sweden exist because the kings of Sweden encouraged careful town planning during the seventeenth and eighteenth centuries. North of the southern highlands is Svealand. This name means "land of the Swedes." Svealand has rolling hills, lakes and plains. The land slopes eastward from a plateau in the west to a narrow coastal plain along the Baltic Sea.

The large island of Gotland, northeast of Oland, is part of central Sweden. Vishy, a town on the island, dates from the Middle Ages. The Middle Ages were from about A.D. 500 to 1500. More than 150 original structures still exist and some of them are very well preserved. Gotland's natural beauty includes unusual limestone rock formations and a great many wildflowers.

Stockholm, Sweden's capital and largest city, is near the eastern coast of Svealand. Stockholm has been called the Venice of the North, because there is water everywhere. The city is built on fourteen islands that lie between Lake Malrean and the Baltic Sea. Nearby is an archipelago of 24,000 islands. These islands are often called Stockholm's pearl necklace.

Stockholm is a beautiful cosmopolitan city with very clean streets. This city and its fine neighboring provinces make up the most populated region of the country. A large number of suburbs surround the city. During summer months many residents leave the city for their vacation cottages on peninsulas and islands.

There are several large lakes in central Sweden. North of lakes Hjalmaren and Malaren are fertile plains. Going northwest, the land changes to forested hills and valleys and then to mountains at the Norwegian border.

Dalama, in north central Sweden, is known as the Folklore District. Summertime is celebrated with many festivals. Villagers dress in traditional costumes, perform folk dances and provide open-air entertainment. Farms and meadows cover much of the southeastern corner of Dalarna.

Norrland, northern Sweden, occupies three-fifths of the nation's land. There are vast stretches of wilderness where no one lives. The far north is above the Arctic Circle. In Arctic lands the Sun never sets completely in summer months and it can't be seen at all during most of the winter. Arctic regions are named "Lands of the Midnight Sun."

Swedish people and tourists from other countries like to hike, hunt, fish, ski and climb mountains in Norrland. Winds from the southwest blow over the North Sea and the mountain range, often pouring heavy rainfalls on Sweden.

Swift rivers flowing from the mountains cut broad, deep valleys on their way to the Baltic Sea. East of the mountains is a band of rolling hills. Forests of pine, spruce and birch exist nearby wetlands and peat bogs. The slopes are lower and gentler toward the eastern border near Finland. The flatlands are swampy in summertime. Forests cover more than half of Norrland. Almost all the rest of the area is uncultivated mountains and bogs.

From May to August, the weather is usually calm and Sunny in Sweden. Days are long and temperature levels are almost ideal. The average temperature is around 68 degrees F, sometimes rising to as warm as 86 degrees F. The hours of Sunlight begin to decrease in September and leaves turn to lovely autumn shades. Frost usually begins in October and snow falls in November in Sweden. During winter the ground is covered with snow and the temperature will stay below freezing.

NORWAY

Norway is a long, narrow country in Scandinavia. Two-thirds of Norway is mountainous. There are more than 160,000 lakes and many islands in the northern country. Ancient glaciers scoured its land and coastlines with the movements of tremendous masses of ice, earth and rock. The glaciers shaped the peaks into such odd forms that they have provoked images of trolls and supernatural spirits. The mountains in the south, which contain the highest peaks in Europe north of the Alps, are called Jotunheimen or Realm of the Giants. A few mountains are so steep that no one has ever attempted to scale them. The 2,000 foot Reka in northern

Norway has never been climbed. The Troll Wall in Romadal (Western Norway) was first climbed in 1967.

The fjords of Norway are sometimes deeper even than the North Sea, although they are often shallower near the coast where the ice sheet is thinner. The Norwegians have divided their country into five main regions according to geography and dialects. Vestlandet (West Country), Oslander (East Country), Sorlandet (South Country) and Trondelag (Mid-Norway) makes up the rest.

In Southern Norway, Sorlandet, the smallest region, is located at the southernmost point. The other three main regions of the south have wide mountain barriers. Where the southern half of Norway ends, northern Norway or Nord-Norge begins.

Vestlandet has well-kept villages and coastal towns nestled against a backdrop of majestic mountains. The West Country is the representation of Norway best known to the rest of the world as picturesque Norway. This narrow coastal zone reaches into the Atlantic Ocean and has many islands and steep-walled narrow fjords cutting deeply into the interior mountain region.

Sorlandet has idyllic coastline that has become Norway's foremost summer vacation area. The land is hilly, but the agricultural season is slightly longer than in Oslo, Norway's capital. The interior of Sorlandet with its narrow valleys running up into the beginnings of Lanfjellene is very sparsely populated. The people in the different settlements there depend on dairy farming, sheep raising and forestry.

Ostlandet's East Country has more than half of Norway's population, who live mainly in and around the metropolis of Oslo and in the region around Oslofjord. This area is mostly urban and industrial. There is also agriculture which is found mainly in the lowlands extending eastward and southward toward the Swedish border. The lowlands are well cultivated because of enough rain, rich soil and the highest summer temperatures in Norway.

The largest forests in Norway are found between the Swedish border and the Glama River, east of Oslo. The coastline near Denmark across the Skagerrak Pass, stretching from Oslofjord to the southern tip of Norway, is densely populated and crowded with small towns and villages.

About half of Oslandet is covered with forests. This region has a little more than half of Norway's total forest resources and a share of Norway's cultivated land. Oslandet is where mining and manufacturing industries exist.

Trondelag is centered around the long Tarondheimfjord. Trondheim, the region's major city, is the third largest in Norway. Trondelag has less industrial development than Oslandet and Vestlandet because there are few suitable sites for power stations. There is a small agricultural area on the eastern shore of the fjord.

Nord-Norge has mountains with jagged peaks and ridges. A long string of large islands jutting into the Atlantic west of Vestfjordin forms the Lofaten archipelago. Numerous fjords scissor into this narrow strip of Norway's northern tail. Northern Norway has one of the most irregular coastlines in the world, even more irregular than in the southwest.

Nord-Norge has a rugged frontier quality about it. Nord-Norge has been called "The weather kitchen of Europe." Rain, clouds, mist and fog are characteristic of much of the Norwegian Coast. Gales and squalls add a special effect to the north, which has recorded some of the highest wind speeds in the world. Norway's first meteorological station was established there in 1866.

The Gulf Stream keeps the fjords from freezing. Norway's coastal areas would not enjoy temperature and mild climate year round. There are many green forests beyond the North Cape. On Sunny days Sunbathers enjoy relaxing on the beaches.

Average temperatures for the southern part of Norway near Oslo and Bergen range from freezing in winter to 61degrees F in summer. In northern Norway, the average winter temperature is 23 degrees F and the average summer temperature is about 50 degrees F. Occasionally temperatures have been known to reach as high as 77-86 degrees F.

Norway lies directly in the path of the North Atlantic cyclones, which bring strong winds and frequent changes in weather. Western Norway experiences comparatively cool summers, mild winters and a substantial amount of rain. Eastern Norway experiences warm summers, cold winters and very little rain because it is sheltered by mountains. Norway is a land of the Midnight Sun.

Major cities in Norway are Oslo, the capital and home to about 530,000 people; Bergen, with a population of almost 240,000; and Trondheim, which ranks third with 157,000 people.

Oslo is known as the main center for communications, trade, education, research, industry and transportation. It is also Norway's political and financial heart and its center for international shipping. Oslo was founded by King Harold III around 1050. It became the capital of Norway in the 14ᵗʰ Century.

Bergen is the natural center of Vestlandet. Bergen has a more international character than any other city in Norway. It was an active trading center of northern Europe since the Middle Ages. Bergen was founded in 1070 by King Olav III. Bergen grew as a fishing and trading port.

Bergen is the second largest city in Norway and it is the principal port on the West Coast, with a considerable merchant fleet, several large shipyards and one of Norway's six universities.

Trondheim is Norway's historical capital. It was founded in 997 by Viking King Olav Tryggvason (ruled 995 to 1000). In the Middle Ages, Trondheim was an important commercial, administrative and religious core. Trondheim has been a research center since 1760, when Norway's Royal Scientific Society founded a museum and research station in this city.

Other cities in Norway are Stavanger in southwest Norway and Tromas, Norway's largest city is north of the Arctic Circle. It is home to the world's leading research organization for the Arctic phenomena.

FAUNA AND FLORA

Reindeer, wolverines, small rodents, lemmings and millions of kittwakes, puffins, guillemots, auks, cormorants and gulls live in Norway. The sea eagle is thriving here. Lakes and marshes are inhabited by cranes, whooper swans, grebes, geese, ducks and other fauna exist in Norway.

Along Norway's coasts are large numbers of seals and whales. Most rivers have fish such as trout and salmon. Norway has about 2,000 species of plants. Thick forests of spruce and pine trees thrive in the glacial valleys of eastern Norway and in the Srondheim region.

Wild berries grow throughout Norway including blueberries, cranberries and cloudberries. Star hyacinth and purple heather thrive in the warmer regions of Norway. Blue anemone and aconite grow near Oslo.

THE VIKINGS

The Vikings are well known in Scandinavia. Vikings settled in Norway, Finland, Sweden, Iceland and Denmark thousands of years ago. They were explorers who traveled in wooden, Viking boats. They traveled to many places in the world. The Vikings discovered Savalbard, the Arctic islands northwest of Norway. Before A.D. 1000 they had settled in all the habitable islands in the North Atlantic, including the Shetlands, the Orkneys, the Faeroe Islands, Iceland and Greenland, which all remained under Norwegain influence for centuries. They also landed on the shores of North America 500 years before Christopher Columbus did.

The Vikings had a reputation of being pirates because of their warlike raids on other European communities that characterized the first 100 years of the Viking Age. Most Norwegians were farmers and fisher folk who went about their lives. Many Norwegians preferred not to be called Vikings.

Viking settlers based their lives on trade and a well organized and high level of architecture and artistry. They settled disputes and made important decisions at law assemblies. Anyone could have an assembly by sending an arrow to a neighboring farm. One man was selected to memorize the laws and was required to answer anyone who asked a legal question by repeating the appropriate law at the assembly.

Viking women did the household work such as cooking, spinning and weaving. They taught their children stories and riddles, orally passing on their traditions. Viking stories called sagas were not written down until the 13th Century.

There was more equality among the sexes in Viking communities than in the rest of Europe at the time. Viking women could own property, could divorce their husbands and were in charge when the men were away. A wife's symbol of authority, which she carried fastened to her belt, was the key to the storage chest. Norway has had an Equal Status Act, equivalent to an Equal Rights Amendment, since 1976.

Scandinavia is a fascinating place to travel to. The five Scandinavian countries are Denmark, Finland, Norway, Sweden and Iceland. Each of these countries has unique as well as common interests and cultures. The landscapes vary to some extent. All of these countries are in upper Europe near the Arctic Circle. The climate varies to some extent in each of these Scandinavian countries. Each country has traditional customs, costumes, food, religious beliefs and historical heritages. They are known for many forests, lakes and mountains in Scandinavia. Many reindeer roam through Scandinavia. Many of the Scandinavians are friendly people who speak at least two or more languages.

SIXTY-ONE

The Big Celebration

Seomay Rogers looked forward to a big celebration at a Hawaiian luau in Waikiki on Oahu Island. She had just moved to Honolulu in Hawaii. She moved there to work as an airline stewardess. She had received her training as an airline hostess. This was her first job serving on Hawaiian Airlines. Seomay rented an apartment overlooking the harbor of Honolulu. She was able to observe Sunrises and Sunsets which were brilliant colors reflecting over the ocean. During the daytime Seomay saw vivid turquoise and blue colors in the ocean. Many boats and kayaks were seen moving in Honolulu and Waikiki harbors.

Honolulu is a busy port city with high rise buildings close to the shore. Waikiki is bustling with harbor restaurants, large hotels and tourist shops. Seomay browsed through the International Market in Waikiki. She purchased a variety of colorful mumu dresses which she tried on. She also bought some leis to match her new dresses. She was able to find some attractive beach shoes and sandals to match her new clothes. She planned to wear one of her mumus to a luau which she planned to attend soon.

Seomay continued to work as an airline stewardess five days a week. She had different work shifts on Hawaiian Airlines. It was her responsibility to help passengers be comfortable and safe. She served snacks and meals to passengers. She also assisted sick passengers, children and anyone who asked questions about the flights. Seomay was gracious and friendly to passengers. She helped passengers feel welcome and comfortable on the different flights.

When Seomay returned to Honolulu she went to her two bedroom apartment overlooking a magnificent view of the Honolulu Harbor. She relaxed and rested from her busy schedule. She thought about the big celebration she would be going to that afternoon.

Seomay dressed in a colorful red and yellow mumu with white flower designs. She put a yellow and white lei around her neck. She wore white beach shoes. She combed her black, long hair. She placed a yellow island flower in her hair. She was ready to go to the Hawaiian luau.

The Hawaiian luau was on Waikiki Beach. Seomay drove her car over to Waikiki and parked it near Waikiki Beach. She locked her car and walked onto the pristine beach. Hawaiians and tourists were gathered near the luau to celebrate. Long tables were on this beach with colorful, plastic tablecloths arranged on them. Beautiful Hawaiian flowers were displayed on ten, long tables. Benches were arranged around each table. The tables were placed in parallel positions.

Seomay witnessed Hawaiian men and women near a big pit covered with palm leaves. Inside this big pit were roasting pigs.

Pork would be served with poi, rice, green salad, cut tropical fruit and Hawaiian punch. Hawaiian men and women unwrapped the roasted pigs. They carved the pig meat and placed the cooked pork on large trays.

The Hawaiian food was placed on a large buffet table. When everything was ready the guests were asked to line up and each guest was served roasted pork, rice, green salad, cut, tropical fruit and poi. They walked over to the tables with their food. They sat down to eat the succulent pork and Hawaiian food.

Seomay sat at one of the tables near some Hawaiian men and women once she was served her meal. She tasted the pork, which was very tasty. She tried the poi. It tasted like glue. So, she didn't eat anymore of the poi. She ate sliced pineapple and mangoes which were delicious. She ate her green salad and rice. Then she sipped some Hawaiian punch.

While she ate Seomay listened to other guests at her table. She heard a Hawaiian woman sitting nearby say, "The pork is good." Another woman, who was a tourist from America, asked, "Why was the pork cooked in the ground?" A Hawaiian woman replied, "This is the traditional way pork is cooked in Hawaii. We use leaves to cover and wrap the pork so it will cook much better on hot stones in the ground. Early Hawaiians didn't have modern ovens.

Hawaiian music was performed by Hawaiian entertainers. Ukuleles and drums were played while Hawaiian lullabies and folk songs were Sung by several Hawaiian performers. Then six Hawaiian women, dressed in traditional, Hawaiian costumes, danced Hawaiian-style dances. They moved their arms and hands and legs gracefully in a group. Their Hawaiian dancing was very entertaining.

Everyone enjoyed the Hawaiian music and dancing. Then a Hawaiian performer demonstrated blowing fire out of his mouth. The audience responded by cheering him. More Hawaiian songs were Sung this time by the guests with the help of a Hawaiian singer. They sang several favorite, Hawaiian songs. The audience was encouraged to get up and dance Hawaiian-style.

Seomay had a wonderful time at this big celebration. She planned to go to more luaus in the future.

— SIXTY-TWO —

Peaceful Living

Our lives should be meaningful. We need to develop goals and purposes to live by in our daily existence. Without goals and purposes our lives become meaningless and aimless.

What kind of goals and purposes can we develop? People can develop goals as follows. To promote the desire to love ourselves and others, to develop interests, hobbies and talents; to become skillful and educated in order to choose an interesting occupation; to maintain good health by eating nutritious food and to exercise regularly; to expand one's awareness of the world and different cultures, to develop religious values; and to develop self responsibility and moral standards.

Positive attitudes and thoughts help us develop positive goals and objectives. We all live more purposeful lives when we develop worthwhile goals and reasons for our behavior. Every goal and purpose we achieve promotes a more meaningful life.

Well educated people have developed meaningful goals in their lives. They maintain high standards in achieving their educational achievements. They continue to receive higher education until they complete a B.A. and higher degrees. College professors must complete a Masters Degree and doctorate before they are qualified to teach college courses.

Some individuals develop skills in sports, technology, wood craft, carpentry and music. Individuals can learn to play the piano, organ, violin, clarinet, trumpet and many other instruments. Mastery of a musical instrument requires step by step practice and effective performances.

We should develop meaningful purposes and goals in life to accomplish what we want to achieve in our daily lives.

SIXTY-THREE

Reasons For Writing

There are many reasons for learning to write. Creative writing is a valuable skill. The reasons for writing are to develop effective, written communications, to develop different styles of writing techniques and to promote worthwhile results in writing diaries, poems, short stories, articles, novels, stageplays, screenplays, reports, theses and documentary writing.

Skillful writers are able to write about many topics and issues and use many writing styles. Well known writers have written novels, stage plays, screenplays, poems, articles and reports. Well known and famous writers may have positive and negative effects on many people. Their books are well known and read by many people.

Ernest Hemingway, who wrote FOR WHOM THE BELL TOLLS and FAREWELL TO ARMS effected readers lives. His characters were interesting and their character description effected readers' attitudes. Emily Barrett Browning wrote descriptive poetry which effected readers' feelings and attitudes.

John Steinbeck was an effective writer. He wrote GRAPES OF WRATH and OF MICE AND MEN. Both of these books were read by many people. GRAPES OF WRATH is about economic injustice. Poor people from Oklahoma were forced out of their homes. They traveled to California and looked for work in the fields. They were offered 5 ½ cents a basket which was very low wages. Then they were deceived when farm owners changed their wages to 2 ½ cents a basket. Some of the workers left and looked for farm work somewhere else. Eventually, some found work and better living conditions elsewhere.

Shakespeare's ROMEO AND JULIET became a classic, romantic tragedy in England. Shakespeare's tragedies and comedies became well known in the Western World. Shakespeare conveyed a specific purpose and message in each of his stageplays. He wrote elegantly and poetically.

Some famous writers have changed history and cultures because of their beliefs, values and significant messages. Socrates in Greece influenced other Greeks to think more deeply. Gautama Buddha wrote

The Eightfold Path. This philosophy changed many people around the world.

An effective writer is capable of developing topics, issues and ideas. He or she wants to write about meaningful ideas, characters and to use descriptive words and images. Writers are able to be creative and they can communicate their deepest thoughts and they can express their attitudes and feelings about life.

SIXTY-FOUR

Other Dimensions

Other dimensions exist beyond the physical world and physical plane. These dimensions are invisible to the physical eyes. Only the astral eye can see invisible planes. The All Seeing Eye can see even more invisible realities.

Our universe exists in different dimensions. There is an invisible universe within the physical universe. The cosmos has many dimensions. We have seven bodies. Our invisible bodies are the I Am Presence, Christ Self, Soul Presence, Christ Self, Soul Presence, mental body, emotional body and astral body. The physical body is the only visible body. The universe and cosmos is protected and affected by the invisible, existing dimensions.

Other dimensions, which are invisible, vibrate at a much faster rate. Vibrant colors are spectacular throughout the cosmos. Invisible planets exist because they are ascended planets. Purple, green, pink, gold and white colors exist in each galaxy.

Other dimensions help hold the physical universe together. The Cosmic Plan exists in all dimensions to maintain balance, equilibrium and centralization. Every form has a center point.

Concentric rings exist. Electric impulses function in living things.

Cosmic dimensions affect one another. Each dimension was created for a purpose. The law of cause and effect exists in all dimensions. Other dimensions continue to function and operate even though they are invisible.

—— SIXTY-FIVE ——

Fiesta Time

Fiesta time is a special experience for many people who want to have a good time. People dress up in fiesta costumes. They enjoy marching in parades. Fiesta foods are prepared so visitors can enjoy delicious varieties of food.

During fiestas, musicians play musical instruments. They sing fiesta songs. Many people like to dance in the streets to celebrate. Fiestas take place at specific places and times.

People look forward to attending fiestas in Santa Barbara, Arroyo Grande, Salinas, Monterey and San Francisco. Fiestas are planned months in advance. Floats for parades are prepared long before each parade.

Booths are set up so fast food, trinkets, jewelry, clothing, art work and crafts can be displayed to sell during the fiesta. Many people participate at fiestas.

Fiestas usually last for several days and nights. Performances take place during the day and night so audiences are entertained. The purpose for a fiesta is to celebrate and to have a good time.

SIXTY-SIX

An Interesting Conversation

Interesting conversations occur when individuals want to communicate about stimulating topics and issues. Individuals are capable of expressing ideas and they are able to give examples while they have conversations. They may refer to ideas and information from books, magazines and newspapers as they discuss topics and issues.

Chairman Coleman went to lunch with a friend, Marian Kellerman. Charmaine and Marian had known each other in college. They had graduated from college several years ago. They enjoyed discussing ideas about many topics and issues.

Marian and Charmain met at their favorite restaurant called Pete's. They were escorted to a table near a large window with a view of the local lake. Once the ladies were seated the hostess handed them menus. Marian and Charmaine studied the menus. They selected certain entrees. Marian selected roasted chicken with rice pilaf and asparagus. Charmaine selected prime ribs and red potatoes with string beans. Dinner rolls with butter were served. The ladies had herb tea with their meals.

Charmaine began talking about the Masons after she nibbled her roast chicken and ate some rice and asparagus. Charmaine looked intently at Marian. She said, "Did you know the Freemasons are the early leaders who formed the American government?" Marian responded, "Who were the early Masons?" Charmaine answered, "Early American Masons were George Washington, Benjamin Franklin, John Adams, John Hancock and many others who were America's forefathers."

Marian and Charmaine continued eating their restaurant food. They enjoyed their food. The lake was a deep blue. Mist was hovering over the lake. Evergreen trees surrounded the lake. Squirrels were climbing up and down nearby pine trees.

Marian asked, "What did the early Masons believe in?" Charmaine replied, "The early Masons believed in democracy. They wanted freedom, liberty and justice for the early Americans." Marian responded, "Why were they called Masons?" Charmaine answered, "Early Masons in Europe were stone builders. They did mason work. So they were called Masons. They met secretly and formed bylaws to promote freedom of Mason workers in Europe."

Marian raised her eyebrows and she had an inquisitive expression on her face. She finally spoke. She asked, "Were the Masons powerful in Europe?" Charmaine replied, "They were powerful in a secretive manner. They worked quietly and had secret meetings. Members were carefully selected after going through a special initiation." Marian asked, "Why did they meet secretly?" Charmaine replied, "They met secretly to protect themselves from conspiracies and corrupt individuals."

Marian looked bewildered. She asked, "What conspiracies and corruption could affect the Masons?" Charmaine replied, "Other groups existed who promoted conspiracies in Europe. Bankers, politicians and businessmen were corrupt.. They didn't want the Masons to become powerful. Masons joined the Crusades as Knights Templar to defend people who wanted to be free and who were Christians.

Charmaine and Marian finished their dinners. They were ready for dessert. Charmaine had strawberry ice-cream. Marian had custard with sprinkled cinnamon. The women sipped their herb tea. They continued to observe the splendid view from the big bay window. Marian thought about what Charmaine spoke about the Masons. She knew about the Crusaders and how they fought in the name of Christianity.

Charmaine continued, "The Masons, who were Knights Templar, believed in the Holy Grail during the Middle Ages. They believed this cup was used at The Last Supper when Jesus was present." Marian's eyes lit up. She asked, "Was the Holy Grail ever found?" Charmaine replied, "It is believed that the early Christians preserved the Holy Grail. Some people believe the Holy Grail was taken out of Israel and hidden because it was so valuable."

Marian appeared interested about Charmaine's comments. She realized that Charmaine was alert and aware about history. She enjoyed the conversation. She looked forward to seeing her friend Charmaine again to have more interesting conversations.

SIXTY-SEVEN

Acting On Impulses

People act on sudden impulses when they are frightened, angry or in love. People act on impulse when they aren't calm and are not reasoning well. They act quickly and say things they normally would not say and do if they took time to think and calm down.

Charles Bickman was an emotional person. He reacted quickly and very emotionally about daily situations and circumstances. He acted on sudden impulses. Charles reacted strongly with anger when anyone called him disrespectful names and belittled him. He fought with anyone who displayed emotional outbursts.

Burt Tyler knew Charles Bickman. They often saw each other at a bar in their neighborhood. Burt went to the local bar to drink some beers. Burt played pool in the bar. He often won pool games when he competed with other people in the bar. If anyone began to win he could react in a negative way. One night Charles Bickman decided to play pool with Burt Tyler. Charles was a skillful, pool player. He was winning the pool games. Burt became angry. He didn't want to lose the pool game.

Burt slammed his pool stick on the pool table as he tried to hit pool balls. Charles continued hitting most of the balls into the holes. When three balls were still on the pool table Burt tried to hit each of them into the holes. He missed all three balls. Then Charles aimed at each of these pool balls. He hit each of them and each ball went into the holes

Burt became very angry. He took his pool stick and he struck Charles with it. Charles defended himself. He took his pool stick and struck Burt with it. Charles and Burt used their pool sticks like swords to fight. They swung the pool sticks swiftly back and forth for at least five minutes. Finally, Charles hit Burt's pool stick out of his hand. Burt became defenseless. Charles hit Burt with his pool stick and knocked him out because he was very angry. He acted on impulse to have the upper hand in this fight.

Burt was unconscious and he was injured because Charles hit him hard with his pool stick. Other people in the bar witnessed the fight between Charles and Burt. They observed how angry Charles and Burt were. They knew these men acted badly and they were foolish to fight because of a pool game.

Burt was a bad sport. He couldn't accept losing a pool game. Charles was reacting because Burt was attacking him. Both men were impulsive. This fight could have been avoided if one of them walked away. Charles should have stopped fighting. He didn't have to hit Burt with his pool stick. He wanted to hit Burt to get even with him for having a negative outburst during the pool game.

Negative outbursts don't solve problems. Problems can be solved by reasoning and maintaining self control and respect for others. Self respect and spiritual introspection will help individuals to control their negative impulses.

SIXTY-EIGHT

Dealing With Bi-Polar People

Bi-polar people have sudden mood changes. They may appear calm and collected at one moment. Then they may become very moody, despondent and even violent suddenly. Some bi-polar individuals are maniac depressive by temperament. The least little thing or circumstance may tick them off. Doctors prescribe Valium or some calming drugs to help these individuals to control their sudden, emotional reactions and outbursts.

Tyrone McBride was a bi-polar person. He had sudden mood swings at home and on his job. If his wife asked him to help around the house he had negative reactions and sudden moody reactions. He didn't want to empty the garbage or help wash the dinner dishes.

Tyrone often responded in a negative way when his boss, Pete Jackson, ordered him to do certain duties and work at his job as a bricklayer. He was bored with his job because bricklaying was very repetitive. Tyrone wished he could quit his job. However, he had a wife and four children to support financially. He needed to work to pay the bills. So, he had no choice. He had to work to survive.

Tyrone only completed high school. He didn't go to college to further his opportunities to get a better and more interesting job. He was limited in what he could do for a living. He had been a bricklayer for 20 years. Tyrone was depressed while he worked day after day laying bricks all day. He felt trapped in a dull and unadventurous lifestyle.

Bricklaying was a way of life for Tyrone since he was 17 years old. He was 37 years old and he felt he had little to show for all these years. He felt he was uneducated and ignorant. He was depressed because his life was meaningless.

Nicole McBride, who was Tyrone's wife, looked after their four children who were 12, 10, 8 and 6 years old. She cooked all the meals for her family. Nicole cleaned house and shopped for groceries. She paid the family bills with the mutual checking account. She depended on her husband's bi-monthly paycheck to pay for the household expenses.

Each month Nicole tried to balance the joint account. Nicole often economized so the essential bills could be paid. Nicole didn't want any checks to bounce. Tyrone let Nicole do the banking.

Tyrone often came home from work tired and grouchy. He took his frustration out on Nicole and his children. His bi-polar tendencies created a negative reaction in his wife and children. Nicole tried to remain silent when Tyrone had an emotional outburst. She knew if she remained calm and quiet Tyrone would eventually calm down. She had learned that silence was golden. If she reacted verbally in a negative manner Tyrone would act much worse. He would react in a negative manner much longer.

Nicole told their children to leave the room when their father was having a negative outburst. Once Tyrone rested and ate dinner he generally calmed down. He watched television after dinner. Nicole allowed him to select the television programs. Tyrone selected mystery programs and cowboy movies.

Nicole had to cope with Tyrone's negative moods. She wished he would take Valium to calm down. Tyrone refused to take any medication to calm down. Nicole put the children to bed by 9 p.m. She went to bed at 9:30 p.m. Tyrone fell asleep in his chair near the television set. He finally came to bed by 11:30 p.m. or 12 a.m. Nicole was asleep. Tyrone woke her up to have sex. She allowed him to release himself. She hoped he would feel better after making love. Tyrone fell asleep shortly after he had sex with Nicole. She pretended to enjoy sex.

Nicole had lost respect for her husband because of his frequent emotional outbursts. She tried to tolerate his bi-polar reactions on a daily basis. Nicole prayed to God to protect her and her children. She wished she could leave her husband. But, Nicole depended on Tyrone to support her and their children. She felt trapped in a marriage that was unfulfilling and turbulent.

Nicole was afraid that Tyrone might hit her and injure her. She lived with a sense of fear and insecurity. She wished Tyrone would be willing to see a psychiatrist. However, he refused to seek counseling.

Finally, one day when Tyrone came home from work he was in the worst mood he had ever been in. He took his frustration out on Nicole. He blamed her for his problems. Nicole walked out of the living room where Tyrone was having his negative outburst. Tyrone followed her. He brutally hit her and slapped her face. Nicole fell down on the ground.

Nicole began crying. She was hurting because Tyrone was violent. Tyrone hit Nicole several more times. Finally, a neighbor came over when he saw Tyrone hitting Nicole in the backyard. The neighbor pushed Tyrone away from Nicole. He said, "Leave your wife alone! You shouldn't be hitting her! I am going to call the police"

Tyrone was lying on the ground. He knew the neighbor was strong enough to push him away from Nicole. The neighbor, who was called Ben, helped Nicole off the ground. He took her next door to his house. He had known her for years because they were neighbors. Ben took a rag and cleaned Nicole's face. He tried to calm her down.

Nicole realized that she couldn't live with her husband, Tyrone any longer. She asked Ben to help her pack. She used his phone to call her parents. Her parents were willing to let Nicole and her four children live at their house. Nicole was glad she had a place to go. She packed a suitcase for herself. She then packed her children's clothes in other suitcases.

Ben drove Nicole and her children to her parents' home to live. Nicole thanked Ben for his help. Nicole knew she could never go back to her husband again. His bi-polar outbursts were too dangerous.

SIXTY-NINE

Working To Promote World Peace

Humanity should band together to promote world peace. Different organizations have been formed to promote peace, such as the United Nations, the League of Nations and the Peace Corp. These organizations want brotherhood and service to be established around the world.

CARE is another world organization which provides food and other supplies to needy people who are starving and homeless. CARE also promotes world peace. The United Nations represents most of the nations and countries in the world. The United Nations has regular international assemblies to promote goodwill, service and peace around the world.

Democracy has spread around the world. Democracy is a government based on freedom, justice and liberty for everyone. America is trying to liberate the Middle Eastern countries. Democratic governments are being promoted in different Middle Eastern countries. Americans want peace and freedom to exist around the world.

The Peace Corps promotes goodwill and peace especially to needy people in impoverished countries. Representatives work for the Peace Corps. Peace Corps workers teach needy people how to plant gardens and how to become self sufficient. Peace Corps workers live near the needy people in order to help them survive. Needy people learn to become farmers, fishermen, builders and promoters of peace and goodwill

Every person who works for the good of humanity and world peace is serving the world. World peace is possible when people are willing to promote harmony and unity.

—— SEVENTY ——

Knowledge About
The Philippine Islands

The Philippine Islands are one of the most unusual and exciting countries in the Far East. The Philippines are made up of some seven thousand islands. It is the only Christian nation in Asia.

Filipino people are good looking. They are related to the Malaya and Indonesians. There are thousands of Christian churches in the Philippines. It is only in the Muslim south that mosques and minarets can be seen.

Many Filipinos have Spanish names. The Spanish language is not widely spoken in the Philippine Islands. Filipinos are the third largest English speaking people in the world.

The Philippines have a unique culture which is a blend of Malay, Indian, Chinese, Spanish and American influences. This fascinating mixture of Asian and Western cultures, customs, traditions and way of life has certainly made the Philippines a land where East meets West.

The Philippines lie at the western rim of the Pacific Ocean about 500 miles off the coast of Southeast Asia. These islands are north of the Equator, between latitudes 4 degrees North and 11 degrees north. It is made up of some seven thousand islands and islets. About one-third of the islands have names. Many of the rest are either rocks or coral reefs. Less than one thousand islands are inhabited. Only eleven of them make up about ninety-six percent of the total land area of the Philippines.

This archipelago of tropical islands is scattered over the distance of 1,100 miles from north to south. It forms a triangle with the Batanes Islands in the north as its topmost point and the Sulu Islands and the island of Mindanao in the south as its base. Two of the largest islands are Luzon in the north and Mindanao in the south. Luzon has an area of 40,420 square miles while Mindanao has an area of 36,537 square miles. Between them in the Visayan Sea, are the islands known as the Visayas. They include the larger and more important islands of Samar, Masbate, Leyte, Bohol, Cebu, Negros and Panay. To the west are the Caomion Islands and the long narrow island of Palwan. In the extreme south are the Sulu Islands which stretch out like stepping-stones between the Zamboanga Peninsula of Mindanao and the Malaysian State of Saboh on the island of Borneo.

To the north of the Philippines lies the island of Taiwan. To its south are Borneo and the islands of Indonesia. Across the South China Sea to the west lies the southeastern coast of Asia. To the east is the Pacific Ocean, the largest ocean in the world, stretching over one-third of the Earth's surface to the western shores of North and South America.

The Philippines were named in the sixteenth century after King Phillip II of Spain. They became a Spanish colony for almost three and a half centuries. This explains why most of the people today have Spanish names and are Roman Catholics. Their manners, culture and buildings reflect the long years of Spanish influence. To this day the country's currency is the peso which is made up of one hundred centavos.

Fifty years of American rule, in the first half of the twentieth century, has given the Philippines its American system of education and its style of democracy. The English language became widespread and American music, basketball, hamburgers and hot dogs became popular.

The Philippines became independent from the United States of America on July 4, 1946 after the Second World War. It became the Republic of the Philippines. Numerous local languages and dialects are spoken in the Philippines. Filipino has become the country's national language. Filipino is based on Tagalog, a local language spoken in central Luzon.

The Philippines coastline is one of the longest in the world. The country's irregular shape has also provided it with numerous peninsulas, islets, bays, gulfs and straits and as many as sixty-one natural harbors. Manila Bay in Luzon is among one of the world's finest natural harbors. On its eastern shore is Manila, the nation's capital.

The sea is widely felt throughout the Philippines, in the climate as well as in the way of life of the islanders. The sea is warm, clear, calm and gentle as it washes the white, sandy beaches of many of the Philippine Islands. It is fierce and violent when churned up by tropical storms.

The waters between the islands are not deep and are easily crossed when there are no storms. The sea to the west of the Philippines is more shallow than the much deeper waters of the Pacific to the east.

The islands are of volcanic origins and the eruption of underwater volcanoes during prehistoric times lifted the ocean floor so that the tops of submarine mountains jutted out of the sea to form the islands. Even now some islands still rise or sink during volcanic eruptions.

Most of the larger islands of the Philippines have a rugged land mass with mountains running in the same general direction as the islands, from north to south. The highest peak is Mount Apo in Mindanao. It is an active volcano, rising to the height of 9,690 feet above sea level. Mount Pulog is sacred to the tribes in the northwestern mountains in the Philippines. This volcano, near the town of Legazpi in southeastern Luzon, has the world's most perfect cone. Mayon is considered by the Filipinos to be the "angriest" volcano. It has a record number of eruptions. The most recent eruption was in 1978.

The most interesting volcano in the Philippines is Taal. It is believed to be the lowest volcano in the world. It is located in the middle of Lake Taal, south of Manila. It has another, deeper lake within its own crater. Taal's occasional eruptions have caused much destruction in the surrounding area.

The Philippines has at least fifty volcanoes, at least ten of which are active. They are located along a major fault zone, where the layers of rock are broken, which runs across the archipelago from Lingayen Gulf on the western coast of Luzon to Leyte in the Visayas and then south through eastern Mindanao. This zone is part of the "chain of fire" that runs along the borders of the Pacific Ocean, from the Aleutian Islands (off Alaska) down to Tierra del Fuego (at the tip of the South American Continent) and up to New Zealand, Indonesia, the Philippines and Japan. Four-fifths of the world's active volcanoes are found along this "chain of fire."

Earthquakes are common in the Philippines; but many are too weak to be felt. Fortunately severe earthquakes and tidal waves do not occur frequently. Along the fault zone, to the east of Mindanao Island, lies the Mindanao Trench. At 34,118 feet, it is six times deeper than the Grand Canyon in the United States of America. The Mariana Trench is the only other spot on the ocean floor which is deeper. It lies off the island of Guam in the Pacific Ocean.

Lowlands are scarce in the Philippines. The most important is the Central Plain of Luzon, north of Manila, which is the main rice producing area of the Philippines. Other lowlands are formed by valleys and by the narrow coastal plains of the numerous islands. A vast system of rivers flows through the plains and valleys. They irrigate the land and also serve as waterways. The longest rivers in Luzon are the Rio Grande de Cagayon, the Rio Grande de Pampaga and the Agno. Those of Mindanao include the Agusan and the Rio Grande de Mindanao. Rio Grande is Spanish for "great river."

Because of its high rainfall, the Philippines has a large number of lakes, rushing mountain streams and cascading waterfalls. Its largest lake is Laguna de Bay, southeast of Manila. It is actually a lake. Shaped like a fractured heart, it covers an area of 350 square miles. To the southeast of Laguna de Bay is the well known Pagsanjan Falls, the favorite destination of tourists who want to experience the thrill of "shooting the rapids" with local boatmen in their long, narrow barcas or flat-bottomed boats.

Another interesting area in the Philippines is the Chocolate Hills of Bohol. Bohol is the island to the east of Cebu Island in the central Visayas. The Chocolate Hills, found in the center of Bohol, consist of hundreds of rounded grass-covered mounds. These mounds---the result of erosion—are between 300 and 1,000 feet in height. They are green for several months of the year. During the hot, dry season, the grass turns brown. The name Chocolate Hills comes from the brown color. According to a local legend, these hills were formed when huge teardrops fell from the eyes of an unhappy, weeping giant.

The Philippines also has one famous man-made landmark. This is the Banaue rice terraces, north of Mount Pulog, in northwestern Luzon. These rice terraces, 6,000 feet up in the Luzon Mountains, were built more than two thousand years ago by the Ifugao tribe. Their strong, tanned descendants cultivated the rice terraces.

Looking like giant staircases, the green and brown rice terraces encircle whole mountains, covering an area of some 4,000 square miles. They are a special sight. Filipinos think the Banaue rice terraces are the eighth wonder of the world.

The Philippines has a tropical climate which is usually hot and humid all year round. There are two seasons---the dry and the wet. The average temperature is about 81 degrees Fahrenheit, except in the mountains where it is much cooler.

Typhoons occur in the Philippines. There are fierce, tropical storms that blow in from the Pacific Ocean which bring strong winds and heavy rainfall. The Philippines are one of the most typhoon prone areas in the world. An average of about twenty typhoons hit the northern and central parts of the Philippines every year, especially between the months of August and October. Known locally as bagyas, these typhoons cause disastrous floods, damage to property and loss of life.

Abundant rainfall and constant heat has caused a great variety of plants to grow in the Philippines. There are orchids and many flowering plants as well as dense, evergreen forests. Along the coasts are the mangrove swamps and coconut groves where many species of pines grow on the mountain slopes. Bamboo, banana trees, palms such as the sago, nipah and betel and other trees are valued for their ti.

Animals found in the Philippines are deer, wild pigs, wild cats, mongooses, otters and monkeys. The caraboo or water buffalo are commonly seen helping farmers in their fields. There is the tomarao which looks like a small water buffalo. It has horns and it is very wild and dangerous. It is found in the dense jungles on the highlands of Mindanao Island which lies due south of Manila Bay. The tarsier is a small monkey with a head and body measuring about six inches. It has a long tail and large eyes. Its head can make a 180 degree turn to look at whatever is directly behind it. The tarsier lives high up in the trees. It comes out only at night to hunt smaller animals for food. Tarsiers are found on islands of volcanic origin, mainly in the forests of Bohol, Leyte, Samar and Mindanao

There are many species of butterflies, insects, lizards and snakes. There are 750 species of birds. There is the monkey-eating eagle known as the haribon. It is found only in the mountain ranges in the northeastern part of Luzon, and in some parts of Mindanao and Palawian. It has a wingspan of six feet. It is said to be the largest and fiercest eagle in the world.

The Philippine Islands contain a variety of seafood, corals, shells and tropical fish. The Sulu Sea in the far south is famous for its pearls and its many varieties of beautiful and rare sea shells which are widely sought by collectors from all over the world.

The world's smallest fish, believed to be found nowhere else on Earth, swim in Lake Buhi, not far from Mount Mayon in southeastern Luzon. These tiny fish are called tabios. They are very small---about the size of a grain of rice.

The Philippines are divided into seventy-three provinces, with the smallest unit in each province being the village. Life in the rural areas and the villages has not changed much over the years. Agriculture, along with fishing and forestry, provides a living for the people. The island of Luzon, in the north, has most of the cultivated lands. It is also the most densely populated island. Mindanao, in the south, is the least developed.

The Philippines grow crops such as rice, sugarcane and coconuts. Most of the farms are small. The hard life and poverty of peasant farmers in many areas have resulted in a steady drift of people, especially the young, to the cities to look for work.

Manila, the present capital, is the most important city in the Philippines. It is the seat of government and center of the nation. Manila began as a port and trading center at the mouth of the Pasig River which flows from Laguna de Bay into Manila Bay. Today it covers an area of 245 square miles along the eastern shore of Manila Bay, on both sides of Pasig River.

Davao, at the head of Davao Gulf in the southeastern part of Mindanao Island, is the fourth largest city in the Philippines. It is the center of Mindanao's agriculture, logging and mining industries. It is known for fruits such as pomelos, bananas, mangosteens and especially durians, considered by many an Asian as the "King" of all tropical fruits.

Bagnio, 155 miles north of Manila, is the nation's summer capital. It is 5,000 feet up in the mountains and it is cool all the year round. Tourists and residents go to Bagnio to be in a cooler climate.

Descendants mainly came from the Malayans. Today's Filipinos are made up of a fascinating mixture of races. There are a mixture of Chinese, Arabs, Indians, Spaniards, Americans, Japanese and Europeans. Many people are the descendants of Filipinos married to Spaniards. Descendants of Filipinos married to Chinese and later to Americans. Mestizos (people of mixed race) are usually fairer than their fellow Filipinos, often with the best features inherited from either one or both parents. Some Mexicans who settled in the Philippines during the 250 year period of "Manila galleon" trade, also added an Aztec-Spanish strain to the racial composition of the people.

Not all Filipinos are of mixed ancestry. There are curly-haired, dark-skinned Negritos who may be the original inhabitants of the Philippines. They make up at least ten percent of the country's population. There are mountain people of northern Luzon, known collectively as the Igorats. They consist of five main tribes---the Ifugaos whose ancestors built the Bontocs who today combine their ancient religion with the teachings of American missionaries, the Benquets, the Kalingas and the Apayaos. They retreated into the mountains of northern Luzon, when many settlers and conquerors came to the Philippines.

The Muslims or Moros of Mindanao and the Sulu Archipelago form the largest minority group. Among the most interesting tribes of Muslims are the Bajao, the Maranao and the Tausug. The Bajao are sea gypsies, who spend their entire lives on their floating boat homes. They are the true "wanderers of the Sulu Seas." The Maranao are the people of Lake Lanao on Mindanao. They are very . Their brass containers, wood-carvings and brightly colored malongs (tubular women's' dresses) are well known. The Tausug or "people of the current" form the main group of Muslims in the south. They live on the island of Jolo in the Sulu Archipelago and around the port of Zamboanga in the southwestern part of Mindanao. They are fiercely independent. Their ancestors were the first Filipinos to become Muslims.

Other minority groups live in the south. They include non-Muslim tribes who live in the remote highlands of Mindanao. Among them are the Tiluray, a horse riding people of southwestern

Mindanao and the Tbali, a tribe living near Lake Cibu in the Cotabato province of Mindanao.

The Filipinos of northern Luzon are, in general, considered to be shrewd and hard-working. Those from central and southern Luzon are more enterprising and seem to be happiest when in the company of others. The Visayans are well-known for their kind and generous nature. Filipinos from different parts of the Philippines have a variety of manners, customs, attitudes and values. This variety of characteristics, together with the physical differences between the Filipinos themselves, has not divided the people as much as the different dialects that they speak. Around seventy-seven or more local languages are spoken in the Philippines. The two official languages today are Filipino and English. Filipino, based on Tagalog, is the country's national language. Filipino is taught today in Philippine schools. It is hoped that the greater use of Filipino will help to strengthen the bond among the Filipino people.